The Curse of the Snake Princess

By

Michele Roger

The Curse of the Snake Princess

Chapter 1: No Love

Jessica could feel his warm breath on the back of her neck as his fingers slowly discovered the buttons of her sweater. It may have been early May in Michigan, but the heat from their two bodies made the lovers impervious to the plummeting fall temperatures. Jessica turned and pulled Adam closer until her mouth found his. He kissed her hard. She was eager, too. She whispered between kisses, "Did you bring the blanket?"

Adam reluctantly pulled his body from hers to turn and reveal a rolled up sleeping bag from his backpack. "I brought everything. Tonight is going to be perfect," he assured her. "No parents, no curfew, just you, me, the beach and the moon."

Jessica bit her lip. "Did you remember the condoms?" As soon as she said it, she was grateful for the cover of night. The intensity of her embarrassment immediately tightened her stomach, and she felt a wave of nausea wash over her. She pursed her lips together. Adam surely would have seen it if they had more than the moon and stars to illuminate their faces.

Adam held up two purple packets confidently between his index and middle finger. "Stole them from my brother," he announced proudly.

Jessica crossed one foot over the other, sheepishly. She and Adam had been dating for just shy of four months and had spent the last two weeks planning their secret meeting on Belle Isle. She watched Adam as he smoothed out the blanket and placed the packages of condoms on the corner. He returned to her, taking her in his arms. A nervous shiver ran through Jessica's body, and she trembled. "We'll go slow like we planned," he whispered. "I love you," he added.

"I love you, too," she sighed, burying her head in his chest. She felt like she was standing on a cliff, high above a village below. She had left the people and places she had known that afternoon as a person who had only known herself in all the ways that were intimate and private. By morning, she knew she would be different. She was not sure how, exactly, but to offer access to her body in a way no one had ever explored or touched her was guaranteed to change her.

For all the shyness that she felt looking at the condom packets, it seemed to melt away the minute they were in each other's arms. She kissed Adam gently, at first. As their lips lingered, the desire grew.

Jessica's head swam with a wanting she had never known before. Her heart beat so hard she thought it might burst from her chest.

"Ok," she heard Adam breathlessly say in her ear. "Like we planned."

Reluctantly, she stopped kissing him, but smiled. This was it. She loved him so much in that moment. He wanted it to be special for her. So many of her friends' boyfriends had never given any thought at all to their first time.

"I'll be right back," she said with a nervous giggle.

Jessica left the soft sand of the beach and stepped over tall sea grass, making her way to the tree line. Her fingers trembled with nerves and cold as she took off her sweater and shimmied off her jeans. She nearly fell over and laughed at herself as she struggled to hurriedly remove her sneakers and socks. Jessica heard the rustling of the brush in the darkness. "No peeking," she scolded. "Besides, I'm ready." She shivered and returned to the sandy beach where she stood with her arms across her breasts. Her teeth chattered as she called Adam's name.

Saplings just beyond the edge of the moonlight moved. She bit her bottom lip as she threw away her shyness, revealing her body and uncovering her breasts. Adam stepped into the light and gave her a smoldering smile. He offered his hand to her, and she took it. He kissed her as he pulled her to him, and Jessica was grateful for the warmth of his body against hers.

Resisting their nerves and the cold, they ran to the blanket hand in hand, and the two fell onto the sleeping bag. Their bodies entwined. Nervous laughter was exchanged for breathless desire. Jessica gave a small moan as Adam kissed her neck. His lips headed south, making his way slowly down her torso.

Wanting became Jessica's entire world. She entangled her fingers in his hair with one hand and gripped the edges of the sleeping bag with the other. She thrust her hips upward, inviting him in. Adam had reached her torso and he heard her hiss. Her fingers felt his head jerk upwards. "That's an interesting sound," he laughed.

"What?" Jessica asked breathlessly.

Adam was not listening anymore. She heard the crinkling of plastic and opened her eyes to see Adam kneeling over her. "Ready?"

She smiled and took in a deep breath. She sat up and kissed him, helping him as they fumbled with the unfamiliar protection. He pressed his lips to hers and the two of them lay back down, their two bodies becoming one as their passion rose. She wanted him and pulled his hips into her body. She heard him moan. She looked at him and Adam's face suddenly contorted, instantly changing from a look of pleasure to one of agony. He gritted his teeth. Jessica gripped his arms, "Am I doing it wrong?"

Instead of answering, Adam screamed.

Jessica's heart leapt into her throat. Something was wrong with Adam. She was suddenly aware of the sand moving under the flannel blanket. She tried to sit up, but she was trapped under Adam's rigid body. It felt as if every muscle in his legs and arms were iron bars, pinning her to the ground as he jerked and cried out. She fought to break free. Then she felt a searing hot pain in her left foot.

She heard her own scream join Adam's.

Her logical mind struggled to make sense of it. Jessica's train of thought blurred as the feeling of something cold and leathery brushed past her arm. She tried to gasp but it was hard to breathe. Adam stopped screaming and his muscles were trading in their tension for the sensation of his full, heavy weight on her.

With all her strength, she rolled his body to the left of her and was met with a chorus of hissing. Adam's face stared up to the sky, his eyes blank. As Jessica watched, Adam's eyes began turning a milky white. Jessica sobbed in uneven jerks, but her fear told her to run. She stepped hard on the moving blanket, her clumsy feet feebly attempted to propel her to safety. The searing pain hit her hard again in the calf and then again in the thigh.

The moonlight was becoming blurry, and she felt her body stiffen under the power of the moving, slithering beach. Her knees collapsed under her, and she fell to the ground.

Jessica willed herself to blink. The moon was walking towards her. The moon, she thought as struggled to take a breath, was beautiful. As it grew closer, Jessica realized it was not the moon but a girl not much older than herself. Jessica tried to reach out a hand to her, but her muscles had long ago stopped listening to her brain. The poison was in control. Her plea for help was merely a breath as her jaws locked.

The mysteriously beautiful girl stood before Jessica as if bathed in a robe of white light. Three feathers graced her head like a crown. Jessica knelt before the princess as she struggled to take in one last breath. The feathered princess waved her hand and the snakes obediently gathered at her feet like dogs.

As Jessica made her final exhalation, she heard the princess whisper, "There is no room for love here on my island."

The words echoed in Jessica's ears and her body fell over sideways. Her innocent face plummeted into the sand as her eyes turned the milky white color of the moon.

Chapter 2: No Time to Waste

An early evening spring breeze blew gently through the curtains of Mrs. Sidway's dining room window, making the flames of the seance candles on the table flicker and dance. Amanda had not planned to call her mother, inviting her to the Coven meeting, of course, but her mother and the witches of the group had been long time friends. She was not the only one grieving, she reminded herself. The breeze picked up slightly at the sound of Victoria's voice and the candle in front of Amanda blew out.

With all that magic in the room, Victoria was easily summoned. Laughter soon erupted from the women around the table and Amanda watched, aghast as her mother, even as a ghost, elevated the party. Victoria was a force of nature even when she was dead. Amanda confessed, if only to herself, that she missed the mischievous, overbearing woman.

She had questions.

So. Many. Questions about the house left to her, Henri, Victoria's familiar and at one point, lover, until she turned him into a cat.

Moreover, she had questions about the spells Victoria had cast on her and the Sheriff in town. Her first Michigan winter in years and the repairs on the house after fighting the Dogman and his pack of werewolves had torn the old farmhouse as well as her love life apart.

She and Victoria had never been close so why did she miss her mother now that she was gone? Fits of giggles erupted from the room and Amanda reminded herself that apparently, Victoria, at least the party-ghost incarnation, was alive and well. It did not make her feel any better.

Despite the whoops and cheers of the gathering, Amanda's mind wandered from the coven meeting. Her mind recalled the image of a tarot reading she had given herself when she felt snowed in and lonely a few months back. Moving images had played in her mind like a movie with the flipping of each card. A green wooded forest, the smell of the water and moss nearby, and Ashton holding her hand as they walked together, his gentle eyes glancing down at her and giving her a wink. As the vision expanded, she saw they were both wearing wedding bands.

Spring had arrived and the snow had melted throughout most of the wooded areas near town and still nothing close to this vision had come true. Amanda did not expect it to be so, especially because in her reading, she and Ashton had been married. Nevertheless, she ached for the bliss of what she had seen. She and Ashton had fallen a bit for each other while fighting and defeating the legendary Dogman last fall. Still, she wished the relationship would move to the next step. She could not help but wonder if their heat had been the result of

Victoria's enchanted baked goods and nothing more. Since her mother's death, Amanda and Ashton had cooled.

She debated asking one of the witches for a love spell. Sure, Victoria had been baking (and feeding) enchanted baked goods to both Ashton and Amanda since Amanda had arrived back home to their small town in northern Michigan. Now, her mother was gone, at least physically. Amanda had magical inclinations on occasion, but she was not really sure her true magical vocation after a lifetime of stifling them. Love had never been her strong suit and she did not want to lose Ashton. On the contrary, she wanted more.

"It's not the same without you!" Jane Sidway, a retired teacher and longtime of friend of Victoria's exclaimed. "Coven meetings aren't nearly as delicious."

"In more ways than one," Yvonne Sheraton added. "We haven't had a naked man in the garden since you left." The whole coven began laughing and Amanda joined them. "We're just waiting for this one," she pointed to Amanda, "to discover her gifts. Then, we can start sneaking summoning cakes to the men of town again."

The ghostly face of Victoria stared back at Amanda with a hopeful look. Amanda knew she had always been a disappointment to her mother when it came to magical things. Growing up, the need to be "normal" had been more important to her. She wished she had not moved so far away for so long but there was no going back. Magic could do a lot of things, but it could not turn back time. Amanda just returned a small shrug to Victoria.

"How is it, you know, the spirit world," asked April, a kitchen witch.

"Oh, you know, I can't tell you that. It breaks the rules," Victoria scolded. Then the ghostly woman cupped her hands and whispered, "boring." The women broke into fits of laughter once again.

Amanda yawned and stood up, "It's getting late and I have workmen coming over to finish the library in the morning."

"What gives," said Mrs. Sidway. "Why don't you enchant one of those handsome fellows to show up here next full moon?"

Amanda snorted, "Why don't you hire him or one of the other dozen men finishing the renovations to come over here and fix your rickety fence? Enchant him yourself." With that she went to the foyer and put on her coat and hat and headed for the front door. She felt her pocket vibrate with a text. It was Ashton.

"Are you dancing naked under the moon?"

"Nah. The coven is lovely but they're not the people I want to be dancing naked with," she replied. "Heading home," she added. She opened the door and standing on Mrs. Sidway's stoop was a annoyed and grumbling Tom cat. A familiar voice interrupted her thoughts of a naked Ashton dancing in her bedroom.

"This is completely unacceptable!" Henri declared. "Victoria never would have left me under such circumstances."

"I've only been gone two hours and Jimmy was there. Did you walk all the way over here just to yell at me? I left the two of you with anchovy pizza, and a blazing fire in the fireplace. Having your own personal man servant isn't good enough?" Amanda argued. "What more could you want? And let's not forget, Victoria did in fact leave you often when she went to her coven meetings."

Henri the cat growled. "I was a kitten then, really. My life was laissez-faire when she was mine." He swooned dramatically on to the sidewalk for effect. "Now I'm doomed to a life of cheap take-out and binge watching old episodes of Wild Kingdom by myself."

"Jimmy watches Wild Kingdom?" Amanda asked, skeptical.

"No. He watches wrestling. I think I know the reason Jimmy is twenty-eight and still single," replied the cat.

"He works a lot. If that's how he wants to spend his free time, we shouldn't judge" Amanda countered.

"And speaking of working," Henri continued to press his case. "What if Jimmy gets called out on to a case while he's watching me? What if he's gone for hours and forgets to feed me? What if the pipes freeze and there's no water? What if I freeze to death in that ramshackle you call a house?" The cat jumped onto a fence ledge to get a closer vantage point to argue.

"Henri, stop it! I know you're lonely. I know you miss Victoria. In my own weird way, I do too. But Ashton and Jimmy work crazy hours because they must, not because they want to. They're the only law enforcement in the entire County. Everyone has been snowed in for months. It makes people crazy. It even makes *cats* crazy." She stared at him to drive home the point.

"Are you trying to convince you or me?" Henri said. "I have a good mind to throw up a hair ball in your new designer snow boots for suggesting my mental state is in question. I'm grieving." He put emphasis on the last word.

"We're all grieving and if you take to revenge puking there's always boarding you at the vet," Amanda warned him. "For a week."

At the sound of the dreaded "v" word, Henri returned her stony gaze and threw up an anchovy. "I'm not kidding," he added. Then, he bounded off down the street and scrambled across a lawn quickly, disappearing into the dark.

Amanda's phone vibrated again. "Home yet? I just don't like my girl walking home alone in the dark."

She typed back. "Henri checked on me. I'm nearly there.

"That was nice of him."

"He had a list of complaints."

"He's still not taking it well?" Ashton surmised.

"Nope," Amanda answered, pulling a piece of strawberry licorice from her pocket and popping it in her mouth.

"I should be walking you home. Sorry I've been so busy with work."

"You can make it up to me. :)

"I've been thinking about that exact thing. I'd like to take you away for a weekend," Ashton typed after a few minutes.

Somewhere tropical she hoped. Then, she realized that anywhere would be nice as long as she was with him. She wanted to tell him that but instead she wrote," That sounds fantastic. Where did you have in mind?"

Ashton did not text back until Amanda reached the bottom step of her front porch. "Sorry. Had to watch a suspect. Turned out to be nothing."

Amanda wrote back. "Should I pack a bikini? In case there's an ocean?"

"How about a hot tub?"

"Close enough." Amanda headed into the kitchen to make a cup of coffee. She set down the phone.

"Traveling together?" Henri asked as he lay on the counter in the kitchen, reading her phone.

"Think of all the wrestling you and Jimmy can watch together."

"Excuse me while I go puke in your boots," snapped the cat.

An idea popped into Amanda's head. "Why not teach Jimmy how to be romantic? You were once a dashing young man. Instead of My Fair Lady, it can be "My Fair Jimmy." Henri's eyes narrowed at the possibility.

"You're saying I need a project," Henri said, rubbing his head on a coffee cup and rolling on the counter.

"Now, where did mom keep the suitcases," Amanda asked.

The next morning, Amanda awoke to the sound of an engine, and she felt her heart beat a little faster. She recognized the sound of the old Bronco police truck and threw off the covers despite the chill in the house. By the time she made her way downstairs, Aston was inside. He grinned and his boyishly good looks immediately melted any real frustration Amanda might have felt the night before about his lack of presence.

Heavy-pawed padding announced Henri's arrival into the kitchen from the back door. He had heard Ashton too. The cat meowed. To Ashton it sounded like a meow. To Amanda it was, "Tell him I have a few questions to ask about Jimmy's recent and past love life."

"No," Amanda replied.

Henri jumped up on the counter with dirty paws. He'd been in the garden mousing. He purred and rubbed against Amanda's coffee cup. "Ask him or I'll bring the mouse I just killed into your bed when you're not looking."

Amanda smiled sweetly, picking up Henri. She set the cat back outside the kitchen door. There she saw the dead mouse. She quickly shut the door and locked the cat door at the base. Henri meowed from outside in protest, but she ignored him. Instead, she went over and wrapped her arms around Ashton. He held her, bringing her closer to his body and she heard as he took in a deep breath, smelling the fresh scent of her hair.

He pulled away and gave her a smile that met his eyes. He looked tired but happy to see her. "I've got something for you," he said.

"Hang on," she stopped him. "Did you eat? I could whip you up some eggs."

"Later," he said as he tugged her hand and lead her to the front room. There, on the coffee table sat a bouquet of flowers and a small box. The box, mind you, was not small enough to be a ring like what Amanda saw in her cards. In any case, it was a gift box and she jumped at the surprise.

"What's all this?" Amanda asked. She knew that Mrs. Sandalwood always closed her flower shop from January until May, just in time to reopen for Mother's Day. Ashton would have had to drive three towns south to get a bouquet of grocery store flowers and these were an upgrade. He'd driven at least an hour, one way just to buy these kinds of beauties. She picked them up, closed her eyes and smelled them. "Oh Ashton, thank you. They're gorgeous." She set them down. "Can I open the box?" Ashton nodded. Amanda gingerly picked up the velvet covered box. She opened it. Inside was a metal hair clip featuring a Celtic knot.

"It's the closest thing I could get to something witchy," he shrugged.

She hugged him again. "I love it. Thank you."

Ashton leaned in and kissed her. "I know I haven't been around very much and you've got all this renovation going on after the Dogman. Plus," he paused, and his gaze softened, "I know you miss Victoria. I just wanted to do something nice." He shrugged again.

Her stomach fluttered and her heart beat a bit faster.

Amanda put the clip in her long, red hair. She went to the kitchen to put the flowers in water. She expertly cut and arranged them and returned to the front room to place them back on the coffee table. Ashton had taken a spot on the couch, his muscular arm stretched across the back. Henri stared at him with disdain. The cat meowed at Amanda, "He didn't bring anything for me."

Amanda rolled her eyes and sat next to Ashton. His eyes were closed. Did he really not know she was next to him? Of course, he had been up all night on a stakeout. She sighed, pulled her feet up on the couch and rested her head on his shoulder. She placed her hand on his and he pulled himself from sleep. He pulled away slightly to have a look at the barrette. "That looks really nice. I did well picking that out."

"Your modesty is staggering, Sheriff," Amanda teased. "But thank you for this and the flowers."

"Do you think you can be ready to go away tomorrow or is that too soon?" Ashton asked.

"If I can have Jimmy stay here with Henri, then I can leave tomorrow. The foreman has a key so they can keep working while I'm away."

"I want you to know that if anything happens to you, I'm going to make sure Jimmy trips over me and hits his head on something heavy," Henri said, interrupting Amanda.

Amanda grunted, thankful that Ashton could not understand what the cat was really saying. She turned to the disgruntled feline, "Ok. You'll be fine," Then she scratched him behind the ears.

Henri continued, "Then once he's unconscious I'm going to eat him. Do you hear me? I'm going to go full primal and eat him!"

Amanda pretended she did not hear Henri and said to Ashton. "I'll find the suitcases and have the day to pack," she said cheerily.

"I'll be *fine*!? What do you mean by *fine*?" Henri meowed.

"Good," Ashton yawned. "Sorry to be a party pooper but I'm going to head to my place and sleep the sleep of the dead." He reached out and gave Henri a few pats on the head before standing up. "I'm sure Jimmy will be happy to have some company," he said to Henri. He turned to Amanda. "See you in the morning. I'll pick you up about eight."

"Happy snoring," she smiled. She kissed him and let her gaze linger for just a few minutes longer. "Sleep well."

Ashton laughed and headed out the door. When the Bronco pulled away, Amanda collapsed on the couch next to the cat in exasperation. "Henri, I love you. But you won't even eat dry cat food if it's been sitting in your bowl more than twenty minutes. The likelihood that you'll be noshing on Jimmy's entrails two days after you've tripped him is so unlikely that it's hilarious."

"I'll do it. I'll eat his liver and then sleep off my food coma by laying in your bed and stealing all of your covers," threatened Henri.

Amanda got up and opened the front door closet where she had last seen the suitcases. There was her favorite yellow one. It was easy to spot on an airline carriage and had the wheels that did a complete three sixty. She pulled her suitcase down to the wood floor. Henri stared at her with a grimace. "Don't forget to cuddle with my furry slippers," she called out as she pulled the suitcase up the stairs.

Chapter Three: No Romance

"We have ten minutes," Ashton whispered in Amanda's ear as he wrapped his arms around her.

"Hmm," Amanda smiled as she stirred her coffee. "Whatever shall we do?" She did not wait for an answer though. Instead, she pulled him to her and kissed him. She felt his fingers play with her long hair as he lingered in the kiss.

He pulled away just enough to catch his breath. "A whole weekend of this," he smiled as he stared into her eyes.

"Are you sure you won't tell me where we're going?" Amanda asked.

Ashton shrugged but the look in his eye was playful.

"Fine," Amanda said. She buttered toast and took half with her as she went upstairs, leaving the other half for Ashton. She double checked her room and then the rest of the upstairs room windows. Since Victoria's encounter with the lethal Dogman (thanks to an open window) Amanda had taken to locking them up before she left to go anywhere. She kissed Henri who was sleeping on her bed and murmured something about cats and food delivery services.

Amanda came back downstairs and went into the library, which she had been practically living in since her house had started renovation. She texted the door code to the foreman of the work crew incase Jimmy had to leave or either of them forgot a key. Her phone rang and she looked at the number. It was Mrs. Sidway.

"Hello Amanda, I just wanted to make sure that you're doing okay. You left early last night. We thought you'd want to see Victoria."

"Oh, I'm fine," Amanda said. "I did see her and I'm grateful to you all."

"You don't fool me. I know you miss her. We loved Victoria but none of us wanted her for our mother," Mrs. Sidway laughed.

"Thank you for checking in on me," Amanda hedged. She did not want to get into an emotional conversation before leaving with Ashton.

"Your abilities will surface. Don't worry," said Mrs. Sidway as if she could read Amanda's mind. "Grief does strange things to us. Be patient with yourself. Have you spent any time in the downstairs room?"

"I haven't," Amanda said truthfully. "I know I promised the ghosts but I'm just not ready. I mean, what if—" she stopped herself.

"What if Victoria comes through," Mrs. Sidway asked.

"Yes. I know it's not my fault, but I feel responsible for the way she died. I should have taken better care of her. I should have done a lot of things better," Amanda said, hearing her voice crack in the process.

"You came back. That's the most important thing. Once you let that go, I bet you'll find your magic. Or it will find you."

"Jimmy's here!" Amanda heard Ashton yell from downstairs.

"Thank you, Jane. I appreciate the advice. I have to go now. Talk soon." She hung up and took a deep breath to steady her nerves.

She was calm by the time she made it to the bottom of the stairs. Jimmy poked his head through the plastic curtain that encased the main room of the house off the kitchen. "Jimmy!" Amanda said, giving the deputy a hug. She and Jimmy had gone to school together and then lost touch when she had moved away to run a bookstore in Chicago. They'd reunited during the Dogman incident and was grateful for his friendship. "I really appreciate you staying with Henri this weekend," she said.

"It's no problem. This way the poor guy won't be so afraid of the workmen," Jimmy said.

She did not have the heart to tell him that it was, in fact the workmen who were terrorized by Henri, particularly when the cat was in a bad mood, which was pretty often lately.

"Almost ready?" Ashton asked.

"All set," she answered.

A car pulled into the driveway and Amanda groaned. "What fresh hell," she muttered under her breath. "I'll be right back."

Ashton gave a little laugh. "I'll put the suitcases in the car."

"The car?" Amanda asked. Didn't he mean truck? Everyone in norther Michigan drove some kind of four wheeled drive vehicle if they wanted to get out of their driveway in January. A car was unthinkable. She answered her own question as she stepped out to see Mrs. Sidway parked on one side of the driveway and Ashton's rental car in the other, a mustang. Amanda stared at the sports car for a moment and thought, "You can take the boy out of Detroit, but you can't take Detroit out of the boy."

Then, she shifted gears. "Mrs. Sidway, is everything ok? Didn't we just speak on the phone?" Amanda asked. She did not want to be rude, but the older woman could be longwinded, and Amanda was seriously beginning to think they would not leave before noon at this rate.

"I'm fine, love," said the older woman. "I just came to bring you this," she unfurled a necklace and pendent and placed it over Amanda's head. "It was your mother's. It will protect you, just in case."

Amanda shuddered slightly. Mrs. Sidway was known for her gift of visions and seeing into the future. "Courage my Dear and all will work out in the end." A breeze blew through Amanda's hair and Jane Sidway looked in its direction. She gave a wry smile. Then, as quickly as the elder woman arrived, she left.

Ashton put the bags in the trunk of the Mustang and met Amanda who was left dumbfounded in the driveway. "What was that all about," he asked.

"Just a little game we witches like to call, "Magic or Crazy?"" Amanda said, rubbing the pendent between her fingers.

"That's pretty. What is it?" Ashton asked, eyeing the new necklace.

"Moonstone. My mother always said it protected the wearer and heightened their magical abilities."

"Cool," Ashton said simply.

The familiar voice of Jimmy drifted into the driveway. Amanda took Ashton's hand and looked surprised to see Jimmy holding Henri in his arms. The cat looked utterly mortified and he struggled to get free. "We'll be fine, won't we Buddy?" Jimmy said to Henri. He nodded to Amanda and Ashton, "You two kids have a good time."

"I really appreciate you staying here and keeping Henri company," she said as she gave Henri a pat on the head.

"What's a good deputy for?" Jimmy teased. "Although, I admit, I always thought the perk of a cat over a dog is that you could fill up their food and water bowl and leave for a weekend and they'd be fine."

Amanda smiled, "Henri isn't your average cat."

"And don't you forget it," Henri scolded. To Ashton and Jimmy it sounded like a meow. The two men stared silently as they watched the woman and the strange feline. Jimmy wondered to himself if all women had one sided conversations with cats or if this was yet another one of Amanda's weird quirks. He was discovering she sure had a lot of them.

Amanda could feel their stares and without warning walked into the house. She returned a minute later complete with her jacket and purse. She handed Jimmy a list of "do's and don'ts" and grabbed Ashton's hand. "Everything packed?" she asked.

"We're all set," Ashton confirmed.

Jimmy looked up from reading his instructions. "Anything else? Nothing on here says 'no feeding after midnight' or anything."

Amanda laughed. "No. He can eat whenever he wants. Just remember, whatever you're eating, he'll want half."

"Not likely!" Amanda heard Henri scoff. "I've seen the crap that he eats."

Amanda smiled as she concealed her ability to hear her familiar and hugged Jimmy. "Thanks for keeping an eye on him and the house."

"No worries. Now get out of here." At that, Jimmy raised his eyebrows at Ashton and gave him a wink. Amanda rolled her eyes and headed for the door. Ashton ran ahead to hold the door for her but stopped to answer his phone.

"Uh huh," Amanda heard him say. She watched him bite the bottom of his lip. He did that when something worried him. He gave Amanda a sideways glance and bit his lip again. "I can be down there in about five hours if traffic is good. Meet you at the station."

Amanda felt her heart deflate as he hung up. "Side trip," he said, trying to sound funny.

"Should I take my stuff back inside?" Amanda asked as she headed for the trunk.

"Nope. This is just a courtesy call. Hank, my friend over in the Detroit precinct has a crime scene he's never seen before. Knowing Hank, that's saying something. He just wants me to take a look, give my opinion and leave. We'll still make our dinner reservations if we leave right now," Ashton said, looking at his watch.

"I imagine this baby could break a few speed limits if it needed to," Amanda said, getting into the Mustang.

Ashton jumped in the driver's seat. "Me? Break speed limits? Why, I'm shocked at what you are implying ma'am."

Jimmy leaned in the window of Amanda's passenger side. "Buckle up. He's wanted one of these ever since he sold his old one."

"How did I never know you once owned a muscle car?" Amanda asked.

Ashton cocked his head and backed the car out of the driveway. The two watched as Jimmy waved goodbye.

"I think you'll find there's a lot you don't know about me," Ashton said, flashing his most devilish grin. He hit the gas and Mustang roared to life.

Chapter Four: No Clue

Amanda leaned her back on the plush leather seat of the Mustang. It was such a change from Ashton's work Bronco and her ancient, red pickup truck. She watched Ashton dreamily as he shifted gears as they headed out onto the I-75 expressway. The ride was so smooth that she would not have guessed they were already doing eighty-five. She saw him give her a sideways glance.

"Radio? Spotify? What's your poison?" Ashton asked, highlighting the screed in the console for her to peruse.

"Actually, this is perfect. I'm just savoring the view," she mused as she watched him. He looked tired. Ashton had been helping the next county over with some stakeout work and it showed in his weary eyes. "Besides, I've heard nothing but hammering and saws since the day after Winter Solstice. Background noise is overrated in my opinion. Unless you want some music to keep you awake."

"I'm fine," Ashton argued.

"You've been working a lot. I don't understand how they can ask you for so much help off the clock." She handed him a sandwich from the bag at her feet. "And clearly you haven't been eating. It's not as good as my mother's but the coven girls sure loved it."

Ashton took the sandwich. "You know I'd be lost without you. I mean that."

It was not wild and crazy love like when Victoria had been feeding them both love spell enchanted cookies, but as she mulled his words over in her head, she decided it was a good start to the trip. The five hour drive included one Bob Seger singing marathon (a pleasant surprise for them both), a deep conversation about how the fate of the world rested on the backs of bees, a story Ashton recalled about being a teenager and outrunning the police in his 1980 Chrysler LeBaron and a power nap taken by Amanda while Ashton listened to the news on a Detroit radio station.

Ashton gently nudged Amanda as they approached Detroit. Amanda had only driven through the outskirts of the city despite living in Michigan all her life outside of the last few years in Chicago. It was a strange mix of old and new, a place trying to remember its glory days one minute and trying to reinvent itself the next. On one block there was fresh, new construction, sleek apartment buildings and new loft housing with crisp, green parks. The next block was the complete opposite filled with burned out homes long abandoned and forgotten, warehouses filled with broken windows and overgrown fields littered with trash and packs of stray dogs. Ashton reached over and held her hand and did not let go when the Bluetooth connected to his phone. Instead, he said, "Answer it."

"What's your ETA," asked a man at the other end of the line.

"We just pulled on to Woodward," Ashton said. "Should we meet you at the station?"

"Meet me on Belle Isle just past the casino. Everything is roped off with yellow tape. You can't miss us. This will be one for our memoirs. Oh, and Ash," the voice added. "Thanks for doing this. I know you had plans with your girl."

"Still do," Ashton said, squeezing Amanda's hand. Ashton turned off Woodward and on to the ramp leading to the island. They crossed the small bridge over the Detroit River. The pale, spring sun fought to shine but its weak light shone nevertheless on the water. Amanda peered out close to her passenger window to get a better look."

"Looking for boats?" Ashton asked.

"Jimmy Hoffa," she teased.

Belle Isle came into view as they passed the Detroit Yacht club and turned right. The casino was less than a minute away. Amanda held her breath when she saw the swirling lights of several police cars as well as the Forensics Lab van and another large vehicle that read WAYNE COUNTY MORGUE. Amanda felt her stomach tense.

"Do you want me to take you to the hotel first?" Ashton asked after looking at the scene.

"No, I'll be fine. I'll just hang out here in the car," she said trying not to look anxious. She honestly wondered if they would make their dinner reservations. There were more police cars at this crime scene than they had in three counties back home.

She heard Ashton sigh. "I'm sorry about this. I'll be as quick as I can. I promise," he said, opening the door and leaving the car running.

Amanda rubbed the pendent necklace nervously. A gust of wind rocked the Mustang and she wished she had worn a heavier sweater. The whole thing reminded her of last November, the Dogman, the Lupin Moon, three victims including one crime scene she had found on her own. There were four victims if she counted her mother. "Oh Victoria," she whispered. "I really could use a chat with you right now."

A cold rainy sound filled the car, like tiny droplets in a spray. Amanda looked around. She shut off the dash screen for fear it was malfunctioning. She sniffed, trying to detect the familiar smell but could not recall it. "I honestly thought that woman would never give that necklace back!," said an exasperated voice in the back seat. Amanda whipped around, jerking her chest with the safety restraint of the seat belt. Amanda fumbled with the seat belt button, cursing quietly at first and then shouting as she struggled to get it undone.

"Well, your vocabulary hasn't improved any since I died," the voice added.

Amanda scrambled to her knees and looked in the back. All she could see was a light, grey mist. She shivered at the freezing temperature of the back of the car. "Mother?!" Amanda found herself whispering.

"Why are you whispering, he's gone. And might I say you two sure could use some help within it comes to conversation. This is supposed to be a romantic weekend, not a documentary on the pollinating habits of insects. My god, did I teach you nothing? And a sandwich, you packed him a sandwich? On plain, un-enchanted bread. After all the work I put into that man *for you*!"

"You know I could never bake like you could," Amanda argued. "And how dare you listen to our conversation? How long have you been listening?"

"Long enough that even I fell asleep, and I'm dead!" Victoria scolded.

Amanda stared at the back seat with the profound fear that she was losing her mind. "You are dead," she whispered again. "None of this is real," she heard herself say and this time, tears threatened to fall.

Victoria's voice was gentle as she replied, "Dead but not gone, my dear. I've been working on Jane Sidway for weeks, coaxing her to return that necklace. It's high time she said goodbye to her husband. He's been gone fifteen years. It's our turn now."

Tears rolled down Amanda's cheeks. "It's you? Like it's really you? At this moment, I think I might need a cat scan."

"Listen to me. What you need to do is get out of this car when Ashton comes looking for you. He's going to need your help on this one. Well, he'll need OUR help but he doesn't need to know that."

"I don't have clearance. It's a secure crime scene," Amanda said, wiping her nose and searching her purse for a tissue.

"Leave that to me."

The temperature inside began to warm slightly the second the mist exited the car. Amanda closed her eyes and did breathing exercises she had read about in a book about grief she had found in the library. She jumped in her seat and gasped when Ashton opened the driver's side car door. His face looked grave and he gave her that look that was all detective. She hated that she knew that look so well.

"I hate to ask, but I need your eyes on this. I've never seen, I mean, I can't explain," he paused. He handed her a badge on a long cord and shook his head, "I need your help." Amanda felt the pendent around her neck grow cold and she knew it was a proverbial kick in the butt from her ghostly mother. Amanda looked around to see the mist but could not see any visual signs of Victoria. Still, the pendent was enough of a sign.

Amanda and Ashton made their way to the crowded crime scene. They walked up to a thin, middle-aged man in his forties, Amanda guessed with dirty blonde hair. "Amanda, this is Hank," Ashton said. "Hank, this is the one I told you about."

"You've been talking about me, eh?" Amanda teased. "All good things I hope," she teased. She offered a hand and shook Hanks.

Hank gave a wary smile. "Nice to finally meet you. I wish it were under better circumstances. Ashton here tells me you've helped him on some strange cases. This one is the strangest I've ever seen." Hank motioned for Amanda and Ashton to follow. Hank lifted the yellow crime scene tape and Amanda ducked under. The pendent felt nearly frozen by the time she reached the bodies of the victims. She held it in her hand to give the skin on her chest a chance to recover.

"Jessica Connolly aged seventeen and Adam Durant also seventeen. They attended Grosse Point High School. From the contents of their belongings, looks like they were here with a night together in mind," Hank cleared his throat as if laying out the details made him uncomfortable. One of the crime scene lab tech's was putting the condom packet found tucked in a blanket into an evidence bag. Amanda stifled a laugh. "According to the preliminary exam, it looks as if someone or something stopped them before any sexual activity took place. If that were it, I'd say it was some crazy, teenage love suicide/homicide pact and ruled it an accident but," he lifted the tarp over the first body, "seems the cause of death was by venom. Snake bites to be exact. Both bodies are covered in them. Forensics will have to run blood samples to identify the type of venom as well as the species of snake."

"That's the reason for the odd patterns in the sand?" Amanda asked.

"That's my guess, but if so, that's a whole lot of snakes. Where would they come from? Belle Isle Parks and Rec hasn't witnessed any significant rise in Massasauga rattlers populations, although they confirmed there are some living here naturally. Those are the only prevalent venomous snakes in the whole lower half of the state," Hank said.

"But the island does have an aquarium. Does that facility also hold any reptiles?" Ashton asked.

"They're closed today. I've left a message for the director to call me as soon as possible," Hank confirmed.

The two men looked over at Amanda after hearing her gasp. Amanda was staring at the face of Jessica Connolly as the morgue photographer snapped pictures of the corpse. "Her eyes," Amanda remarked. "They're white."

"Eyes get cloudy once the heart stops and the organs shut down," Ashton said.

"No. I've seen dead eyes, Ashton. These are different. "Look," Amanda countered.

Ashton joined Amanda. He knelt and looked at the girl's face from different angles. "What the hell caused that?"

"I asked the M.E. the same thing," commented Hank. "They're researching to see if it might be a possible effect of so much venom in the body at the time of death."

"When did they die?" Amanda asked. "Should rigor mortis have set in so quickly? They look like froze while trying to move? Is that normal?"

Hank shook his head. "Rigor mortis sets in six to eight hours after the heart stops. I'm not sure why their bodies are posed that way. Frankly, none of it makes any damned sense. To top it off, the State of Michigan only recently acquired the island from the City of Detroit. But the kids were from Grosse Pointe. So, I've got agencies here from Wayne County, State Police, the city, you name it. Wouldn't it figure, the strangest case I've ever seen and we've got to add a circus to go along with it? That's why I called you, Ashton. I need another pair of impartial eyes."

Ashton looked at his watch, "Why don't we do this. Amanda and I will quietly slip out of here while you deal with the dog and pony show. We've got reservations and we haven't even checked into our room yet. In the morning, we'll do some poking around the aquarium, ask some questions, dig a little."

"Has anyone interviewed the families?" Amanda asked.

Hank rolled his eyes, "You mean besides the damned press? They got to them before any officers did. We've got the Victim's Unit taking their statements now."

Aston patted Hank on the shoulder. Then he took Amanda's hand and the two made their way to the car. Once he started the engine, he shut off the blue tooth. He dialed a number from his phone. "Hi, I have reservation for six thirty," he said. "Right. Can I bump that up to seven thirty? Perfect. Thanks." He hung up the phone.

"Why'd you shut off the hands-free?" Amanda asked.

Ashton looked determined. "Dead teenagers and snakes shouldn't be the only surprise you have tonight. And this isn't how I planned to kick off the weekend." He took her hand and gave it a kiss. "Let's try this again. We'll check in to the hotel and then, a romantic dinner with no ghosts or anything weird."

Amanda felt her pendent get cold and she had to stifle a laugh. Instead, she asked, "Seriously, where are we going?"

"Ok, ok, I've booked us a table for two at the Whitney," Ashton said proudly. "I lived down here for years, and I've never been. Nearly all my friends proposed here."

"Really?" Amanda teased. Ashton realized what he might have implied and shifted uncomfortably in his leather seat. Amanda laughed, "Oh and by the way," she added, "the Whitney is super haunted. Their bar is called The Ghost Bar for a reason."

Chapter Five: No Way

Henri lay on the pillow of the couch watching Jimmy with interest. A large box had arrived that afternoon and Jimmy had finally decided to end Henri's genetically inclined curiosity and open it. "You see," Jimmy explained to Henri as if they were having a perfectly normal conversation, "I read that intelligent animals grieve. Dog, elephants, dolphins, whales and even cats all are sad after the loss of a companion. Then I started wondering what would happen if I got called out on a case when I'm supposed to be here taking care of you."

Jimmy heard Henri meow. What Henri actually said was, "very sensible. I'm glad you see it my way and I'm guessing this means you've reached the same logical conclusion that I have and you've taken some vacation time off to care for me in the manner respectful of a cat."

"So," Jimmy continued, "I got us this!" He pulled a bright yellow backpack from the box and removed the cellophane wrapper. "I can see you're stoked."

Henri's eyes were as wide as pancakes as he stared at the abomination. He meowed, "And what the hell am I supposed to do with that?!" He regretted asking the question the second he meowed it. As if Jimmy understood, the deputy decided to demonstrate instead of talk. Henri was abruptly lifted off of his plush pillow and dropped, feet first into the large pack. He panicked when he heard the top of the pack click.

"There's no escape!" Henri cried out. "I'm going to suffocate in here! This is worse than WWF or terrible food. What's happening?!" He bellowed.

"Don't worry little dude," Jimmy cooed. "I've got you." He tapped on the large, clear plastic bubble window of the pack, conveniently designed for a cat's eye level. Jimmy turned the dial that let in additional ventilated air. "Isn't this great? Now, we can go everywhere together. Let's try it out."

Henri felt is confined world move as Jimmy lifted the pack from the couch and slung it on to his back. "I'm going to kill you," the cat meowed. "There is NO WAY I'm going anywhere in this thing with you! I'm going to kill Amanda for leaving me with an insensitive half-wit."

"Let's head downtown," Jimmy said as Henri watched his world bob up and down in the glass window of the pack. He watched in horror as the door closed behind them and Henri was at the mercy of Jimmy and his backpack debut. "See?" Jimmy said. "Isn't this better than just staying at home or in the garden. It's a whole big world out here and now we can see it together."

Henri growled. "I need streaming services and salmon and massage and a fluffy robe. I like being home. I don't want to be outside. I'm a cat, not a sardine stuffed in a can."

Jimmy put in his earbuds and sang along to the White Stripes, "I just know that we are gonna be friends." He marched towards Patsy's Pasties happily while Henri plotted murder.

Meanwhile, Amanda lay on the bed listening to Ashton whistle in the shower. A small part of her wanted to join him but she hesitated. They'd gone from hot and heavy and slow burn over the winter. A weekend away was a step in a positive direction and she did not want to ruin it. Instead, she pulled out her laptop as she towel dried her own newly showered hair. She typed, 'History of Belle Isle, Michigan.'

She skimmed through the webpage of the Detroit Historical Society but there was no mention of snakes, poisonous or otherwise. She switched angles and researched the effects of snake venom on human bodies. Gruesome images filled the screen as she scrolled, and she shut her laptop with a shudder. Those poor kids. She had to stop thinking about it and focus on getting dressed.

From her suitcase, she pulled out one red dress that showed a bit more leg than she was normally comfortable with as well as a slightly more elegant black dress that accentuated her chest. Both options were a huge upgrade from the jeans and sweaters she had been practically living in since November. She held up one in each hand and considered them.

"Leg or breast, it's hard to choose," Victoria said, making Amanda jump.

"Holy crap, mother, what are you doing here?" Amanda whispered, scolding the apparition.

"I could lie and tell you that I'm here to help you pick which dress to wear tonight on your romantic dinner date," Victoria mused. "But what's the point? You haven't let me pick out a single item of clothing for you since you were three. If I had known I was going to give birth to such a stubborn thing, I would have just gotten a dog. And if I'm being honest, there are better things to look at. I figure if I go invisible, I can watch the man in your shower drop his towel."

"Mother!" Amanda scolded again. The pendent getting colder around her neck the longer Victoria stayed present.

"Why aren't you in there?" Victoria chided. "You *have* slept with him, haven't you?"

Amanda suddenly felt shy. She cautiously glanced at the closed bathroom door. "Twice," she whispered.

"Only twice!?" Victoria shouted. "In all these months?"

"Did you say something, Babe?" Ashton asked from behind the door.

"No," answered Amanda, a little too high pitched. She scrambled around the room, removing the pendent and searching for a place to stash it, hoping it might silence Victoria. Meanwhile, she ghost of her mother watched calmly from her perch on the windowsill. "The spells wore off once there were no more of your enchanted cookies and cake," Amanda admitted. "And there were always work crews around fixing the house after all hell broke loose and he's been on stakeouts," she whispered. "Ok? So backoff!"

"I handed the most edible bachelor in the entire upper peninsula to you on a platter," Victoria folded her arms and scoffed.

"A cake platter," Amanda whispered. "He's going to be done any minute."

"Yes, I know," Victoria smiled wickedly.

"Out!" Amanda commanded.

She ran to her purse and stuffed the pendent into a little velvet drawstring bag where she kept her earbuds when she was not out for a run. The bag had a small protection and invisibility charm that Amanda had managed to conjure to keep them from being stolen. "I banish you to this bag," Amanda whispered. The clasp on the purse clamped shut like a pair of jams, clipping Amanda's finger and making to bleed. Amanda kicked her purse with a barefoot as Ashton opened the bathroom door, sure enough, wrapped in a towel.

"The bathroom is all yours," he announced.

"I'll be ready in a jiffy," Amanda smiled and as she passed him, she stopped to give him a quick kiss.

He gave her a wildly wicked look for just a minute and Amanda wondered if they might skip dinner. Good thing she had locked Victoria in her purse. Instead, he just stared at her, running his finger along her jaw and the side of her cheek. "Thanks for the help today. Tonight, it's all about you and me, ok?"

She beamed and she felt the heat on her face as she flushed. "Which one do you like better, the red or the black. You choose while I finish to get ready.

By the time the two of them, (well three really, Victoria was still in Amanda's purse), made it back to the Mustang, they had twenty minutes to spare to make it to their reservation. "Ghost Bar for a drink?" Amanda suggested.

"Sure," Ashton said. A minute later he asked, "What do you like to drink? I mean, we've shared a beer or two or a glass of wine, but what do you like if we're celebrating?"

Amanda's heart skipped a beat. What were they celebrating, she wondered. "French Seventy-Five," she answered. "All celebrations should include champagne or French vodka. Or both."

"Interesting," was the only thing Ashton replied. It made Amanda a bit uncomfortable but when she looked over at him, he was wearing that mischievous grin, so she set her fears aside and determined to relax. They pulled into the small parking lot at the back of a huge mansion off of Woodward. The sign, in elegant cursive writing read, 'The Whitney.' Amanda thought back to her middle school days and the report she had been assigned about the steel tycoons of the industrial era in Detroit. This had been the residence of one such tycoon back in the day, now preserved and in a constant state of maintenance.

Inside, the lobby was filled with ambient light thanks to a lead crystal chandelier. A hostess took them to an intimate table and place setting near the window overlooking the garden and a water fountain. Ashton nodded his thanks and told the hostess that they'd like a drink in the bar before starting dinner. She gave them directions to the second floor and lead them to the elevator.

The two stepped in and after the doors closed Amanda laughed. "These elevators are tiny compared to modern day. Were people really that much smaller or were elevators just meant to cram people together?" Ashton shrugged and pulled Amanda close to him and kissed her all the way to the second floor. When the bell dinged, he pulled away, leaving her breathless and a little lightheaded. They stepped out into the darkly lit bar with recessed lighting and dark red carpet. A jazz trio was playing softly and Ashton lead Amanda to a small table near the corner. A waitress promptly arrived. Ashton ordered a beer for himself and a French Seventy-Five for Amanda. He frowned and pulled his phone from his pocket. She knew at once that it was something pertaining to the case by the sigh he gave.

"Go answer it. Hank needs you. I'll be fine. Maybe I'll even interview a ghost or two while I'm waiting," Amanda said.

"I won't be long. I promise," Ashton reassured her and headed to the hallway.

The handle on Amanda's purse was cold against her shoulder so she set the bag down on the table. She leaned back into the shadows for fear someone might see her and think she was crazy. In the darker section of the table, Amanda opened her purse and pulled out the little velvet bag. She took out the necklace and pulled it over her head. "Okay. Banishment is over but no more looking at my naked boyfriend. Agreed?"

"Agreed," came a voice next to her that made her jump. Victoria was invisible but her cold energy was enough to make Amanda shiver. "That was a dirty trick you pulled putting me in that bag. Still, I'm pleased to see you've found enough magic inside of yourself to be able to hear me. I suppose that's something. And it's nice to see so many new faces."

Amanda looked around the bar, puzzled. There were four couples. "I wouldn't exactly call it hopping in here tonight."

"I don't mean them, I mean the dead people, dear. I've stuck to the safe zone so to speak of the afterlife, home base where I established the basics."

"I can't resist asking. What are the basics when you're dead? What could you possibly need?"

"Everyone needs a place to feel safe, Amanda. In the afterlife, that place where you rest yourself, as a spirit can be anything, a house, a cabin, under the ocean. Hell, you could live in a teapot if you really wanted to. I made my home in a little place by the ocean. After so many harsh winters, I decided my very soul needed the sea. It was only after you and the coven girls called the other night that I realized I really needed to get out a bit, explore what this side has to offer a spirit."

"There are a lot of ghosts here? Really? I guess this place really is haunted like they say," Amanda said.

"Ghosts like to be around people who are vulnerable. That way, they can enter their bodies and remember what if feels like to be alive, even for a little while. Ever wonder why they called alcohol a 'spirit' or why people act unpredictably when they've had a lot to drink? They are vulnerable to the ghosts in the room. The older a place is in the living world, the more it becomes established in the afterlife world." Amanda paused. "Oh, and by the way, speaking of old houses, our house and the door in the library. You have a bargain to uphold. I have some neighbors who are very upset that they haven't had a chance to tell their story and have it put in the living archives."

"I know. I'm sorry," Amanda said and then stopped as the drinks arrived. The waitress set down a napkin and placed her martini glass down. She did the same for Ashton's drink. Amanda took a sip of hers. It was good. "The last few months were easy. I wasn't ready. It's hard to explain."

A soft and kind laugh came from Victoria. "It's ok to miss your mother. In fact, I think it's natural."

"Yes, well. It was a huge surprise for me so don't rub it in. Why don't you go find some vulnerable person to possess?"

"Put the pendent back in your purse. I won't spy on you and Ashton for the rest of the night. I will, however, be doing a little investigating of my own. This case is fascinating."

"Thank you," Amanda whispered and took another sip from her champagne glass. As she felt Victoria leave, she saw Ashton heading back after his phone call. He rubbed his arms as he sat down.

"They must have the AC cranked up in here. It's cold," Ashton shivered.

Amanda brought her drink back to her lips to hide her smile. Victoria, alive or dead just could not help putting herself as close to a good looking man as she could. Amanda reached out her hand and held his. "Is this any better? Warmer?"

"Not as hot as the elevator but it's certainly nice," Ashton confided. He entwined his fingers with hers and explained, "You were right, it was Hank. The toxicology report confirmed that there were high amounts of rattlesnake venom in both of the victims' bodies. It's been ruled the cause of death. Strangely, the bodies' stiffness as if frozen at the moment of death and the extreme white coloring of the eyes is not a side effect of that type of poisoning. The coroner had no explanation for those two anomalies in either of the kids."

Amanda thought about it and wondered if Victoria was hearing any of it despite her promise to leave the two of them alone. She thought about the trapdoor in the floor of her house and the room with the locked door to the afterlife. She still wore the delicate gold chain with the key to the lock around her neck. Should she go home and open the door? Maybe someone there knew something about the murders. Belle Isle was an island with a lot of unknowns. It had passed hands in ownership, and it did not have any private residences but that was all about she knew. Maybe she could ask Jimmy to look up Belle Isle in the library archives and see what he could find. It would be a good project for him and Henri to bond over.

"Hey, where'd you go?" Ashton asked. "That looks like a hundred mile stare."

"Sorry," Amanda shrugged. "Just thinking about those kids and how I can help. That's all."

He kissed her hand that he was holding and held his beer up with the other. "A toast. To a night off. No more about the case for the night. Tonight, it's just you and me." They clinked glasses. "See any ghosts while I was gone?"

"I did, actually," Amanda said.

"Of course you did. You're a magnet. What did they want?"

"She was interested in my hot boyfriend, but I told them that you're taken," Amanda teased.

"Any word from Jimmy?" Ashton asked after taking a sip of beer.

"Nope. I'm hoping no news is good news. I was just thinking that I should think of some kind of activity for them to bond over if he's going to be the stand-in babysitter."

"Activity, like what?"

Amanda shrugged. "Henri won't venture past the garden now that Victoria is gone so obvious things like fishing or chasing bugs like he used to are out of the question. Henri has taken to binge watching on streaming services."

Amanda could feel an odd sensation on the back of her neck. It was not cold, like Victoria. It was uncomfortable. Her eyes darted towards the bartender, but he was talking to a couple at the bar.

"You okay? Ashton asked.

Amanda took another sip of her drink. "I'm find. Just got a strange feeling." She rolled her eyes. "It's probably just all the hype of this place."

"We wouldn't want you spirited away or anything," Ashton said, standing. "Speaking of which, should we take these drinks downstairs to a slightly more private dinner?"

"I'm starving," Amanda admitted.

As they left to return to the elevator, Amanda noticed a man at the bar was staring at them. He made direct eye contact but did not smile or acknowledge her in a friendly way. "Head downstairs, quickly." Amanda heard Victoria whisper in her ear. Amanda turned and held Ashton's hand a little tighter as the two made their way down to dinner.

Chapter 6: No Explanation

To Amanda's disappointment, the Belle Isle Aquarium did have a reptile section and the sight of so many snakes and lizards made her skin crawl. Three small rooms made up the overall aquarium, the first a showcase of freshwater fish, the second reptiles and the third was a nature center/gift shop of sorts. Ashton wore his badge on his belt, giving him both the presence of authority as well as a slightly more laid back look since he was not in uniform. Either way, Amanda got the distinct impression that Dr. Angela Crane, the Director was not impressed but rather annoyed. She clearly had better things to be doing with her time and did not hide her disdain for the line of questioning that came along with Ashton's visit.

"Our facility is far too small for any kind of breeding program what so ever. We are supplied by our partners," Dr. Crane said dryly.

"Can I get a list of suppliers for the report I need to file?" Ashton asked.

"The Detroit Zoo and the State of Michigan Wildlife Rescue. Their addresses are online," she answered curtly, staring at him over her glasses.

"Right," Amanda heard Ashton say as she left them alone and decided to look around. She could see how the average tourist would find the freshwater fish exhibit interesting.

Most aquariums featured salt water based aquatic life. But Amanda had grown up in Michigan and knew the species well. Since she was not a fan of the reptile room, she decided to peruse the nature center and gift shop. "Maybe I'll find something for Jimmy, a thank you gift for watching Henri. With that thought, she considered calling them to check in. "No news is good news, Amanda," she reminded herself.

"Can I help you," came a sullen voice from around the corner. Amanda looked around and saw a willowy thin girl with coal black hair sitting in the staff break room. "I'm only letting you know I'm here, so you don't steal anything. There IS someone here."

Amanda pinched her eyebrows together at the strange address and said, "No thieves here, just us lowly tourists looking for a thank you gift."

The girl stepped out. "Who are you thanking with a gift from an aquarium?" It was a reasonable question, but the way she asked it made Amanda feel like she had grown a second head.

"My cat sitter?"

"Who babysits a cat?"

"My cat has special needs," Amanda tried to explain and hoped it came across as a joke. The girl just stared at her with loathing. Amanda gave her best forced smile and returned to browsing the limited selection of local honey, mitten shaped key chains and postcards of Detroit icons and architecture. She looked up to see the girl was still watching her. "Still," Amanda tried again, "it must be a nice job to work here and meet people from all over."

"If I'm being honest, I hate people. People lie. They break your heart," she said.

"That's enough, thank you," came a voice from the hallway. Dr Crane stormed into the room, past Amanda and took the girl by the wrist, accompanying her to the staff room. Behind the closed door, Amanda and Ashton could hear the director scold the girl. "If you weren't my daughter, they would have fired you by now. I know you're upset about Jacob but that doesn't give you the right to be rude. If you had taken even five minutes to pay any attention to what's going on, you would have noticed that these people are working with the police!"

Dr. Crane left the staff room and slammed the door behind her. Her demeanor switched to charm, and she asked, "Can I help you find something?"

"I found it. Can you just ring me up?" Amanda asked, trying to sound as friendly as possible. She added, "Being a teenager can be tough."

Dr. Crane scoffed, "The way she's acting you'd think she was the first girl in all the world to have her heart broken. Honestly."

Amanda smiled sympathetically and took her receipt and the book she bought. She and Ashton returned to the car.

"Learn anything?" Amanda asked once they were safely inside and out of ear shot of anyone.

"Scientists are grumpy?" Ashton said wearily.

"That might have more to do with parenting a teenager and less about your line of questioning," Amanda reassured him.

"No. They only have two rattlers, and both are accounted for. No breeding program and no residential structures where any private citizen might be crazy enough to breed them. She said Parks and Rec does a seasonal check, but they can't survey all nine hundred and eighty-two acres of the island. Still, she thinks it's unlikely that the amount of snakes we're suggesting were on the beach at dusk. She thinks they would have been looking for places to sleep for the night."

"Unless something was driving them to the beach, compelling them somehow," Amanda hedged a guess.

"I just have to go down to the substation and file this report then I thought we might have a stroll through the art institute and then the riverwalk?" Ashton asked.

"That sounds nice. Can you pick me up from the hotel though? Since the science line of questioning and Dr. Crane seems to be a dead end, I thought I might ask Jimmy to poke around the archives at home. Maybe there's something on the more paranormal end of things?"

"This I just how cases go Amanda. Sometimes the leads go somewhere, sometimes they don't," Ashton explained.

"I know. I just can't get those eyes out of my head. Besides, this way I'll feel like I'm helping."

Ashton dropped Amanda off at the hotel and headed to the substation. Amanda rang up Jimmy. "Hello?" Jimmy answer, sounding out of breath.

"Hi, just checking in. Everything ok?" Amanda asked.

"Perfect," Jimmy said cheerily. "Henri and I are out for a walk."

Amanda was almost speechless, trying to picture Henri voluntarily out walking. "You mean you somehow got Henri on a leash and outside of the garden? Did you sedate him?"

"Nah," Jimmy laughed. "I just have a way with animals."

Again, Amanda was speechless. There had to be more to the story but maybe it was better she did not ask. "Uh ok. Hey, can you call me when you get back to the house? I need you to look something up."

"Sure, just tell me now and I'll remember."

"Can you go in the state library archives and see if there's anything on legends from Belle Isle or anything to do with people's eyes turning bright white or their bodies freezing in place?"

"Life is never dull since you moved back, I have to say," Jimmy said.

"It's not me this time. It's for a case down here and I figure since we just so happen to have the most detailed state archives of any library in Michigan, why not poke and see if we can help out."

"Right on. Henri and I are on it. I'll call you if I find anything."

"Thanks."

Sitting on the bed, Amanda opened her laptop and typed in the internet search, "Legends of Belle Isle, Michigan." Nearly fifty Detroit based legends popped up, mostly modern ones based on homicides in the city. Finally, she found an entry about the Lady in White. *'White'*, thought Amanda. *'Wonder if anyone's eyes turn white when she's around?'* She clicked the link and read.

"Belle Isle is an island in Southeast Michigan and was developed as a leisure spot for residents of the city as well as travelers in the nineteenth century. According to oral histories handed down through the generations, Native American Chief Sleeping Bear had a daughter that was renowned for her beauty. He grew tired of the requests for her hand in marriage and finally just did not allow her to see any of the suitors who were persistently entering tribal lands in the hopes of gaining a chance to gain favor with her father. To rectify the problem, Chief Sleeping Bear wrapped his daughter in a blanket and put her in a canoe. He sent her and a small group of warriors down the Detroit River, banishing her from the tribe and family."

"The legend continues by saying that the Chief called upon the Great Spirit to protect his daughter. If he was to banish her, she would need a sanctuary. At first, he called upon the wind, but the Wind just blew on her constantly, in love with her body and persistently attempting to swipe away her clothes. Finally, the Great Spirit sent snakes to the island but also granted the princess immortality. Modern day visitors to the island say that the Snake Princess, is dressed in white and wanders the island at night. Belle Isle is both her sanctuary and her curse for all eternity."

"Chief Sleeping Bear's daughter, the princess became known as the Snake Goddess of Belle Isle. Oral history also says that a "Lady in White" has the power to morph into a white doe. There have been several people who have claimed to have witnessed the mystical doe and made police reports about it. Debunkers of the legend say there have been families of fallow deer on the island for years. Several have been white ones. Following the pandemic, when attendance to the Isle was high, Michigan DNR relocated the all the fallow deer were to the Detroit Zoo. Funding was cited as the reason for their removal. Will the Lady in White, the Snake Princess or the White Doe reappear?"

Amanda clicked in the scientific footnotes in the article about the legend. "Before Belle Isle officially was given its name during Detroit's industrial boom, locals referred to the island as Rattlesnake Island. Belle Isle, as well as Bois Blanc Island, another island just north of Belle Isle are notorious for their large concentration of native snakes, although some of them are not rattlers. The most common snake in the area is the native water snake. While specifically a phenomenon limited to springtime behavior, rattlesnakes and water snakes have been known to gather and share breeding spaces. It is unknown if interbreeding takes place."

Amanda sat back on the plush pillows and pinched the bridge of her nose. She wondered why Dr. Crane had not suggested that the beach and its strange marks could have been a breeding episode. Maybe Ashton had not mentioned the details of the crime scene. Her thoughts drifted as she lay back in thought. Had two teenagers, nervous and drunk in love just happened to be at the wrong place at the wrong time? It might be possible.

She fell asleep. It was the deep kind of sleep one did when they were left alone after a night of not sleeping because you did not want to snore, fart, talk or anything else in front of your new lover. And you wanted to touch said lover, but you also did not want to rush things. So, you only half slept the night, too afraid to make an advance and yet too afraid to sleep so soundly you might miss that lover's touch. Amanda settled into the pillows of a newly made bed in the midday sun. She fell into the deep sleep of dreams.

She was a little girl, asking her young, beautiful mother if she could go out and play. "Stay in the garden," Victoria had called out from the library. Then, Amanda was a teenager, sneaking back into the same garden by climbing over the fence, breaking a bra

nch and clumsily falling into a row of cabbages in the vegetable patch. "Amanda," came the stern call from the kitchen window. Teenage Amanda cursed. The light was on. She went to answer but when she did so, her voice was not hers. It was a low, guttural answer that was half words and half growl. Her dreamself looked down at her feet and saw that her high tops had been replaced with huge, hairy bare feet. Her fingers had claws. She was a monster. Entering the kitchen, her monsterself saw Victoria and howled. Victoria ran but the monster ran faster. Her vision turned to red, one part rage, one part blood. As the dream

Amanda propelled herself through the dream, one minute Victoria was there, the next minute, she was dead. "I'm sorry, "her real voice said. "It's my fault," she sobbed, feeling cold. "I'm sorry."

"Amanda!" Victoria's voice sounded in her ears and Amanda bolted upright. Even as a ghost, Victoria could still give Amanda the look that only a mother, afraid for her child could give.

Amanda blinked. She looked around the room trying to get her bearings. She looked at Victoria, reached out to touch her face. Her hand fell through the freezing mist that made up the image of her mother. "Oh mom, I'm sorry," Amanda sobbed. "I should have protected you. That, that thing. It killed you and I didn't stop him in time."

Victoria shook her head no, "Listen to me right now. Wrap up in your blanket, first of all, your teeth are chattering. I apologize for that. Cold is one of the downsides of being dead. Second, might I remind you that cancer had already taken over most of my body. Did you forget what brought you back home? Don't you see? I went out with a fight. I gave everyone downstairs enough time to arrive, to get ready, to do whatever you needed to do and it worked. In the end, you killed a two hundred year old werewolf." She said it like it Amanda deserved an award. "Besides," Victoria added cheerily, "Can you imagine how awful I would have been in Hospice? In the end, I'm not really gone. Here I am thanks to my pendent and your powers."

Amanda looked at her skeptically, with tears. Victoria continued, "What I'm trying to tell you, my darling girl is that you need to stop grieving and get on with your life. I left you a house, a job, one hell of a man and a very lovely cat, my best friend in fact. I'm the one who's dead and you're the one who isn't living." Victoria stood up from the side of the bed and put her hands on her hips. "Now, no more apologies. I've come to warn you about two things. One, Ashton is heading back and you look like hell. You're in desperate need to a shower and a makeover." The ghostly woman cocked her head to one side. "A shower will have to do."

Amanda rolled her eyes, "Thanks."

"Two, the man you saw in the bar, the one who stared straight at you. He's what we in the afterlife we call a Collector." Amanda narrowed her eyes in confusion. Victoria continued, "A Collector is a sort of matchmaker, if you will, for possession. He is a living human who listens, he 'collects' people's stories, their troubles, etc. He seems sympathetic and a listening ear. But he preys on their weaknesses. He meets with a ghost or spirit and sends that spirit to the vulnerable person to take over their body for a certain amount of time."

"Why? What does the Collector get out of it?" Amanda asked, trying to understand the strange arrangement.

"Oh, Collectors get paid alright, in favors and power, both in this life as well as the next. Some theories say that Collectors become demons once they die. I don't really know about that. What I do know is that he took a very keen interest in you last night. Don't go anywhere near him. You're grieving and he can smell it. Do you understand? Stay with Ashton. And for heaven's sake go have some fun. Happiness, love, joy these are all blankets of protection that we wear when we are alive. You're far too young to be sleeping and crying in the middle of the day." Amanda gave combined laugh and a sniff. Victoria stepped back and the necklace appeared on the bed. "Keep my necklace with you at all times. I'll keep an eye out for him."

"Does he have a name," Amanda asked, "this Collector?"

"The others I spoke to refer to him as Raven," Victoria explained. She lifted her head and then gave Amanda and urgent look. "Quickly now, in the shower. Ashton is in the elevator. Don't forget my necklace." Amanda took her mother's advice and adorned the talisman. She headed to the shower before Ashton could see her tears.

A minute later, Ashton unlocked the hotel door. "Amanda," he called.

"In the shower," Amanda answered. "Just getting ready. Sorry. I fell asleep," she admitted. The next thing she knew, Ashton opened the door and poked his head in. She pulled the shower curtain back and smiled, "All good at the station?"

He nodded. "Yep. I did say we'd help out with one interview but more because I thought you'd find it interesting. Then we'll head out on the town. Sound good?" Ashton asked.

"How intriguing, Sheriff. You sure know how to keep a girl interested," she teased. "Who are we interviewing?"

"A psychic rang up Hank and says she has information about the case. She claims she can confirm that it's murder," Ashton said, sounding skeptical. "I figured if anyone is an expert on that end of things, it's you. You don't mind?"

"Oh, I mind, but I fully intend for you to make it up to me," Amanda laughed. She shut the curtain and finished to rinse the conditioner from her hair. 'Time to start living again, Amanda,' she reminded herself.

Chapter 7: No Stopping

Henri was practicing his lion stance and doing his deep breathing in the garden. It was utterly ridiculous that the most common yoga and meditative poses were named after the actions of dogs. There was not a canine within twenty square miles who could stretch, pose or deep breathe like a cat. Why did humans have to get everything so wrong? He had just found a sunbeam and decided that meditation needed a peaceful transition into a nap when he was shaken awake by Jimmy and the back door of the house colliding with the brick.

Jimmy had the dreaded backpack in his hands as he struggled to put on his uniform jacket with his other hand. Jimmy stopped and Henri gave him an annoyed look. How many times could this man test a cat's resolve not to kill a human before nature just took its course? Yesterday the backpack and a humiliating walk into town, today, interrupting his inner peace and meditation. There was only so much a cat would take.

"Let's hit it, little buddy. Merril down at the hardware store caught a couple of kids shoplifting and we have to make a report," Jimmy said.

"Meow," replied Henri but in fact he really said, "Leaving the house AND teenagers? Have a good time. I'll wait here for-

" but the cat was cut off. Jimmy scooped Henri up in his arms and with a whoosh, the sleepy feline found himself back, securely in the backpack, his face conveniently settled at the height of the glass bubble. "Oh no, we're not doing this again," Henri protested. He started to fight his way out of the bag. Jimmy whistled, ignoring his scratching, and tearing with his claws. Henri saw the white and blue paint of the squad car and screamed. "Not the car!!!! Cars can only mean one thing!"

"Strap in partner," Jimmy said calmly. He placed the seatbelt over the backpack and clicked it securely. Then, he started the car. Picking up his mouthpiece he radioed in, "It's Jimmy. Tell Merril I'm heading down to his store now. ETA eight minutes."

Inside the backpack, Henri heaved and panted. His eyes glued to the world just outside the backpack's bubble. That was it, he told himself, he'd smother jimmy in his sleep for sure. Tonight. He did not care if Amanda would likely send him into the forest to be eaten by wolves or whatever super angry witches did to their homicidal cats.

They turned the corner and Henri's heart felt like it might explode from his furry chest. He read the word "Vet" on the sign. His eyes darted to Jimmy but the car did not slow like it normally did. Instead, they continued on to a new place called "Merril's Hardware." An older man was standing outside with a can of bear spray aimed at two teenage boys sitting on the wooden bench on the sidewalk, just outside of the store. Jimmy pulled in and put the car in park. He leaned over to get his notebook and pencil to take a statement when a truck sped past and slammed on the breaks. The two teenagers made a run for it, jumped in the bed of the truck and the driver hit the gas. The tires squealed and Jimmy sat up to watch the truck speed off down Main Street.

Jimmy reached down and switched on the lights and siren of the squad car. He threw the squad car in gear with one hand and hit the gas. With his free hand, he radioed into the station. "This Jimmy. Our two suspects fled the scene in a tan pick up," he read the plate number and gave a description. "Requesting backup," he added.

Henri sat frozen with fear, his claws dug into the nylon interior of the bag. His ears were back and his eyes the size of the moon as he watched, transfixed at the car chase taking place. The truck in front of them turned down Petoskey Lane and gunned it. Jimmy radioed again, "Suspect is headed to the onramp of I-75. Request assistance, over," he said. Jimmy slammed the receiver down and followed the truck, gunning the engine to keep up. The truck swerved like it was going to go onto the highway and at the last minute took a sharp turn it McCormick's soybean field.

Jimmy banked hard right and Henri put his paws over his eyes. He felt Jimmy's arm protectively lean against the backpack for a Monet to protect the bag and the cat from shifting or worse in the intense turn. Henri took it back, if he made it home alive, he would not kill Jimmy. He'd go hide under the bed and never, ever come out. He'd sing reggae in cat meows until people brought him food. It would be a peaceful end of his days. The radio crackled and the voice of older man came through. "Jimmy, it's McCormick. Some idiot is racing his pickup truck through my soybeans. Jack just called to tell me, and Sarah said I could radio you."

Jimmy groaned and lifted the police radio mic. "I'm after them now, McCormick but it's just me. No back up. Tell Jack to keep the horses in the barn til we get over the Sam's place. I think that's where they're headed next."

"I'll make some calls. See if we can get you some help," McCormick replied.

"10-4," Jimmy said, dropping the mouthpiece to concentrate on driving the car through uneven farmland.

The patrol car caught a bit of air as it hit a large bump in the soil. They landed hard. "Left, left!" Henri shouted. "McCormick hasn't cut the wheat around the pond. We're headed straight for it! Left! Left or we'll drown!" To Henri's shock, he felt the car swerve to the left at the last minute. The truck in front of them did not swerve. Barreling through the field, the truck broke through the tall wheat did a nosedive at tremendous speed into McCormick's fishpond. Jimmy slammed on the brakes and skidded the patrol car to a halt.

Jimmy rested his head on the steering wheel for a long time, breathing hard. Then, he stared out the windshield, his hands still white knuckled at ten and two. He was panting from adrenaline. After several long breaths, he stopped to look at Henri in disbelief. Within a few seconds the two could hear Jack and Sam revving their tractors and heading their way in the hopes of pulling the truck from the water. Three teenagers climbed out of the truck's windows and stood on the roof, waving for help. Jimmy finally turned his whole body towards Henri and opened the top flap of the bag. "You. Can. Talk?"

Henri stared through the foggy glass of the backpack, "You can hear me? Usually, only people who really love me can hear me." He shrugged. "Who knew I could give great directions?"

Meanwhile in Detroit, Ashton and Amanda set off in the Mustang towards Belle Isle. "Just a quick interview with this woman," Ashton handed her a card. "She came to the substation and said she information about the case, but Hank doesn't really have time for anything outside of the normal investigative channels. I hope you don't mind. Her office is just across the road from the Island. Then, the Riverwalk?"

Amanda felt her pendent grow cold as she read the name on the card, 'Dr. Kathleen Cumberland.' Victoria must have had an opinion about this psychic, but Amanda suppressed any open channel of communication. She did not think Ashton was ready to know that Victoria was back in their lives. Besides, if she was honest, she was not ready to share Victoria with anyone. Amanda adored how close Victoria and Ashton had been but she was the daughter and she needed her mother. She had know when she could talk to Ashton about it.

They pulled around into a space along the road. Ashton took Amanda's hand, preventing her gently from leaving the car. "How do you want to do this? I should identify myself as an officer but how do you want me to introduce you?"

Amanda smirked, "If she's as psychic as she says, she'll know I'm a witch the minute I step in the room. If not, just be honest and say that we have a meeting immediately following this one." Ashton nodded. He hopped out of the car and opened her door for her. "What's all this," she asked.

"It's the least I can do. This is a whole lot more detective work than I planned for one vacation," Ashton admitted.

Hand in hand they walked up the step to a two story house that had been converted to commercial property. Ashton opened the door and Amanda stepped in. She blinked as her eyes adjusted to the dim lights. The scent of pachouli hung heavy in the air. Amanda nudged Ashton and whispered, "it smells fake."

"Hello?" Ashton called out. An older woman wearing a platinum blonde bob hair cut stepped out from a curtained back room. Ashton held up his badge. "Miss Cumberland? I'm just here to ask you a couple of questions concerning the crime scene yesterday on Belle Isle."

"Doctor," said the woman. "Dr. Cumberland. "I have a doctorate in Metaphysical Studies." She pointed a manicured nail up to the framed diploma on the wall.

"Forgive me," Ashton said. "I didn't mean to be disrespectful, Dr. As I said, I'm just here to ask you a few questions."

Amanda began to stroll around the front window of the lobby where a shelf of gift items and self-help books. She heard Dr. Cumberland clear her throat, "Excuse me, are you with the officer or can I set up an appointment for you?"

"I'm just browsing for the moment. I'm waiting for the detective, actually," Amanda answered truthfully.

Dr. Cumberland ignored Ashton as he opened a notepad and crossed the lobby in quick steps with her arms open. "Oh my dear child, you've recently suffered from a big event in your life. Can I offer you a hug?"

"No thank you," Amanda said and took a step back. Her pendent was nearly frozen against her skin and she had to shift her body to make it move, lest her skin have freezer burn.

"Human to human interaction is the first step to healing," the Dr cooed.

"I think I'll do my interacting verbally. Thank you," Amanda insisted.

"If we could just get to the line of questioning, then we won't take up anymore of your time," Ashton said firmly, placing himself between Amanda and the psychic.

Dr. Cumberland lowered her arms and tilted her head. "Of course," she said softly. "What can I help you with?"

Ashton shot Amanda a questioning look and she gave him a forced smile in return. She willed him her response. She was okay. Just get on with it. Hank clicked his pen and turned to Dr. Cumberland. "So according to my colleague down at the station, you said you had information about the case?"

"Yes, they sent me a message," said the woman.

"Who did?" Ashton asked.

"Those poor children. Their souls are trapped due to the violence of their deaths. They demand justice!" Dr. Cumberland said, dramatically.

"Right," said Ashton. "Do you have any information about who might have killed them?"

"Really, it's their karmic debt that lead to that kind of tragedy. Their enemies from another life have come back to seek their revenge. Adversarial relationship just keep repeating in our many lives until one side is strong enough to break the cycle and make peace."

"Do these adversaries have any names in this life?" Ashton asked keeping a straight face but Amanda began to detect the faintest snark in his voice.

"Well, we could explore that. I could hold a seance for a small fee," the doctor phished.

Ashton closed his book, "I don't think that will be necessary. If you have any additional information pertaining to present day, living citizens, please let me know. We'll be in touch."

Freezing, Amanda was sure that if she exhaled, she would be able to see her breath she was so cold. Why was Victoria standing in front of her when they were clearly getting ready to leave? A creak came from the side door and out stepped a man. Amanda gasped but swallowed hard to suppress her fear.

"Richard," Dr. Cumberland sang, "this is just a detective here from the station asking questions about the unfortunate night on the Isle. Detective, this is my son, Richard."

"And who is this lovely woman? Your partner perhaps?" Richard moved even faster than his mother as he crossed the room to reach Amanda. He reached out his hand to shake Amanda's but a foot away from hers he jerked back as if he were shocked.

Amanda felt braver with Victoria's protection. "Sorry," she said. "My aura is a bit prickly today. Did you say your name was Richard or Raven? I wasn't sure I heard correctly."

"At the sound of the word Rave, the man's beady eyes narrowed. He pulled back and ran a thin hand over his slicked back hair.

"Either is fine," he said, taking several steps away from Amanda and Ashton towards the safety of his own mother but keeping his dark eyes on Amanda.

Ashton rested his hand protectively on his gun with one hand and walked over to Amanda, taking her hand with the other. He said nothing to the pair in the psychic lobby and instead, hurried Amanda outside. He did not say anything until they returned to the safety of the Mustang with the doors locked. He reached in the back of the car and dug his jacket out from a spare bag. "Here, put this on. You're freezing. And while you're getting warm can you please tell me what the hell just happened in there? Who is that guy? How do you know him?"

"I don't," Amanda said, pulling the pendent out from against her skin and setting it on the fabric of her dress. "Not really. He was in the Ghost Bar last night. I noticed he was looking at me and I just got the creeps from him. I heard one of the waitresses call him Raven," she lied.

"Those two are the creepiest people I've ever interviewed and that's saying something," Ashton said, shaking his shoulders as if he were sloughing off a cold rain. "I'm not even going to file a report. I'll just tell Hank it was a dead end."

Amanda closed her eyes and willed herself to calm down. What had Victoria said? She was vulnerable because she was giving in to grief. She had to start living. It was a witches understanding that light attracted light and dark attracted dark. She needed some light in her life again.

"Ashton, can we skip the Riverwalk?," she asked,

"Are you not feeling well? I knew I should have told Hank no."

"No, it's just that I'm ready." She looked at him and she let her eyes send the heat she had nearly forgotten still burned for him.

"I'm ready to feel alive again. There's been so much death and dark." She put her hand on his, "Room service? In bed? Shut off our phones for just tonight?"

Ashton's boyish grin spear wide across his face and he made an illegal U-turn. "Why Miss Burton, are you suggesting that we play a little hooky from this case? Because after whatever that was back there, I sure could use some time just you and me. What did you have in mind?"

"I have a list," Amanda laughed.

Chapter 8: No Precedence

"What's first on the list?" Ashton asked as he let the hotel room door close behind them.

"Sorry?" Amanda asked.

"Your list," he looked at her with mischief in his eyes. "If I remember correctly, couples going away for the weekend are supposed to spend some actual time having fun; getting to know each other again?" He brushed back a wisp of hair from her face and leaned in. He kissed her. This time, instead of pulling away after a minute, a habit she had taken to over the winter, she kissed him back. They stayed that way until finally Ashton lifted his head and the two had to catch their breath.

"You haven't kissed me like that since," he stopped himself.

"Since the days of enchanted cookies," Amanda said, finishing his sentence. "I know. And now you know it's how I really feel, not thanks to some spell."

"I didn't need any love spell to make me fall in love with you," Ashton whispered. "Some things are just meant to be and you're of those things for me. I knew you were grieving after Victoria passed. I just waited and hoped you'd come back eventually. So, what's on this list of yours?"

Amanda smirked. She kissed him again and this time she willed herself to let down the walls of protection that she had built to surround and seclude herself. Her hands clung to Ashton's shirt, pulling him closer to her. He followed her lead as they climbed onto the bed. Passion took over and the night was a sea of skin and pleasure, desire and ecstasy as their two bodies became one. They started out slowly but soon, Amanda lost complete track of time or space.

Sometime in the late morning the next day, Amanda woke to the sensation of Ashton's lips on her neck and his hands caressing her. She blinked as his beautiful face came into focus. "I think we need to get some breakfast," he chuckled as she struggled to shake off the sleep.

Amanda yawned, "Are you hungry?"

"You certainly are. I woke up thinking an animal had gotten into the room. Turns out that your stomach growling," he teased.

Amanda smacked him with a pillow. "What do you expect, we skipped dinner last night."

"And burned a considerable amount of calories in the last eight hours," Ashton added. He got up from the bed and headed to the bathroom. When he returned, he offered her a hand. "Come on, we can take a swim in the tub and then grab some breakfast."

She hesitated. "Just a few more minutes," she grabbed his wrist and pulled him towards the covers. At the same time, she heard her stomach and the two of them laughed. Ashton pushed the covers aside and pulled Amanda by the ankles making her squeal.

He picked her up and fireman's carried her over his shoulder. "It's decided. Come on sleepy head."

By late morning, the two were dressed and sitting inside a little cafe. Amanda absentmindedly thumbed Victoria's pendent as she read the menu. Ashton sipped coffee and placed his hand on hers. "That's new," he said, pulling Amanda from the tough decision between eggs Benedict and a stack of French toast. She looked at him puzzled. "The necklace, it's new?"

"This was Victoria's. It's what Mrs. Sidway stopped in to bring me before we left. Mom had loaned it to her a while back and now she thought I should have it," Amanda explained.

"What does it do?" Ashton asked.

Amanda took a deep breath and wondered if it was the right moment to tell him about the reappearance of Victoria. The decision was made for her as her phone buzzed on the table. Jimmy's name appeared in large letters at the top. Amanda held up her index finger. "Hang on. Jimmy's calling on video."

"That's not like him," Ashton said, wearing a look for concern.

"Hi. Everything ok?" Amanda asked as she answered her phone.

"Uh. I don't know how to answer that exactly," he paused. "I thought maybe there was something wrong with the plumbing because the guys working on the drywall in the living room said there were some strong noises coming from the basement. I know you said never to let anyone in the basement, so I said I'd take care of it. It got so loud this morning that I finally opened the trap door with the extra key you left me in case of emergencies."

"Okay," Amanda said, slowly, taking a deep breath.

"Well, I don't know how to explain it so I figured I'd just show you." Jimmy flipped the phone camera around. Standing in the kitchen were two misty forms, one of Victoria and one of a man with long black hair dressed, well like a Native American. Amanda stared at the screen. Before she could stop him Ashton came to her side of the table and stared.

"Mrs. B," he said, sounding elated. Victoria smiled and waved to Ashton. Then she turned to her ghostly companion and was pointing to the phone. The camera phone flipped back around to a very confused looking Jimmy.

"Did that guy come out of a closet in the cellar?" Amanda asked, concerned.

Jimmy shrugged. "One minute there was all this banging and knocking and singing so I opened the door thinking one of the workmen somehow got in there and locked themselves in. The next thing I knew they were up here. I locked the trap door and tried to talk to them, but Victoria said just to call you." He leaned in closer to the phone and whispered, "What the hell, Amanda, you could have told me there were ghosts in the house. And Mrs. B. How long has she been back?"

"Jimmy, I'm sorry. This is all new to me and Victoria's only been back about forty-eight hours as far as I knew." Amanda glanced up at Ashton and then back to Jimmy. "She thought we might need some help with this case. Can I call you right back?"

"This isn't something where you call me back, Amanda. I need you to tell me what the hell is going on and why are there two ghosts hanging out in the living room?"

Ashton's phone rang and he reluctantly pulled himself away from Jimmy and Amanda, stepping a few feet away to answer. Amanda concentrated on her screen. "Can you put Victoria on the phone?"

"How? It's not like she can hold it!" Jimmy said, clearly rattled by the situation.

"Just set it on the counter," Amanda instructed.

He did so and in a second, whiskers and a set of owl-like, golden eyes peered into the phone. "You should go away more often.

This weekend gets better and better," meowed Henri.

"Henri, put Victoria on the phone, please," Amanda asked. But the car began to rub his face all over the screen and purr.

Ashton returned looking more irritated than Jimmy. "You were right. We should have stayed in bed," he said as he put money on the table and picked up the bill to pay for their breakfast. "We have to go. There's been another homicide and another victim in the hospital in critical condition from snake bites."

"What?" Amanda said, keeping Jimmy on the line as she gathered her things. She heard Victoria scold Henri to get off the counter.

Ashton continued, "You won't believe who the victims are," Ashton said, taking Amanda's hand.

Victoria came through the Bluetooth speaker as Ashton started the Mustang, "Dr. Cumberland has been murdered and her son, the one I warned you about, he's been attacked too. This man," she pointed to the ghost beside her, "is Chief Sleeping Bear. He says that he knows who is committing the murders and wants to turn himself in as an accomplice."

Jimmy took the phone, "Excuse me sheriff, but if someone turns themselves in, aren't I supposed to arrest them? How do I arrest someone who, I'm pretty sure is already dead?"

Ashton stared at the road and shook his head, "Why, why can't we just have a normal homicide? Uh," he paused, trying to figure what to do. He tapped a finger on the steering wheel and glanced at Amanda. Then he said, "Take the Chief's full statement, write it out and send it to me. Put Victoria on the phone."

"Hello, Ashton, dear," said Victoria.

"Mrs. B, you've been in town, but you didn't come to tell me? I gotta say, you broke my heart a bit."

"I'm sorry. There were some things I needed to discuss with Amanda. I'm sure you understand."

"Ok. Well, how about you help me, just like old times. Would that be okay?" Ashton asked, trying to shake off the shock and focus on the case.

"Of course, what can I do?" Victoria said.

"Stand tall and Jimmy, you're my witness. Victoria Burton, according to the Department of Corrections Code of Michigan, Section forty, paragraph seven, I temporarily Deputize you. Do you promise to uphold the law, protect the citizens of your state and report any undoing of said laws?" Ashton asked as he turned down Woodward Ave and joined the throng of police cars parked along the road.

"I do," Victoria said.

"Good. You are in charge of keeping Chief Sleeping Bear from leaving and going, well, wherever it is that people go in the afterlife. He has turned himself in and therefore must give a statement and remain in custody."

"Got it," Victoria said, trying to sound serious but clearly kidding with her new title.

"Jimmy," Aston added, "when you finish that report, send it to Amanda's phone. This is more her neck of the woods."

"So, we're actually going to roll with this?" Jimmy asked.

Ashton looked over at Amanda and softened, "we're absolutely gonna run with it."

"Ok. You're the boss."

Amanda watched as Ashton hung up and gripped the steering wheel, resting his forehead against it and took several deep breaths. Then, he lifted his head and looked at her. "Looks like the band is back together."

"Ashton, I'm sorry. I should have told you about Victoria," Amanda started but he stopped her.

"You should have told me that your mother left the afterlife to warn you about a man who could have potentially hurt you and then," he breathed again to keep calm, "you should have definitely told me when you discovered that man was connected to the case. I'm willing to be opened minded because that's what it takes for us to be together. But you have to be honest with me and tell me what's going on. That's why I'm angry. You could have gotten hurt and it would have been preventable if you had just talked to me."

"I've never been good at the whole sharing thing," she admitted.

"We'll have to talk about that later. Right now I have to talk to Hank and get a look at what we're dealing with. Then, I'm taking you back to the hotel?"

"What?!" Amanda argued.

"Hank will ask me to interview Raven. That man is a threat to you. Victoria saw it and I saw it with my own eyes. Now another person is dead. Do you understand what I'm saying to you? If something happened to you because of my work I'd never be able to live with myself."

"Not even if I haunted you?" Amanda tried easing the tension. "Naked?"

"Not even then," Ashton grumbled but no anger touched his eyes. "Stay. Here. I'll be right back."

Chapter 9: No Way Back

"I'll need to take a statement," Jimmy said, swallowing hard. Interviewing criminals was the part of his job that he hated most. The thought of interviewing dead criminals took his anxiety to new and exciting heights. "For the record, can you please state your name?"

"Chief Sleeping Bear," said the ghostly man. He moved his hands as he said it aloud, one part vocal, one part sign language.

Jimmy wrote it down. "And why have you decided to turn yourself in to the police, Sir? What crime have you committed that you would like to report?"

Chief Sleeping Bear looked solemnly across the room and began, "A man dreams of having a son, a warrior to pass along his knowledge and hand down his role as Chief someday. I went out the night her mother went into the tent to give birth and I asked the Great Spirit for a son. I was greedy. Her mother labored all day and into the night. Grandmother Moon kissed the face of my child just before she left to trade places with the sun. I entered the teepee to find a beautiful flower of a daughter wrapped in skins and sucking. I did not know I could love something so much. As the days grew into weeks and months and years, the tribe also grew to love her. Maybe too much."

"When the Princess was entering her first moon, I noticed that the young men of the tribe did favors for her. They brought her fruits from the forest. They told her stories of their hunts and made her laugh. Soon, other young men from the tribe requested to meet The Princess. Too many visitors made my warriors nervous. How could they know who was a friend and who a foe when they were spotted far off down the shore? My daughter did nothing to dissuade her suitors. Sometimes the young men would visit at the same time. They would fight. I grew tired of it and feared if it continued the situation might bring war to our people. So I told her she must choose a suitor and marry. She refused."

"A chief has an obligation to his daughter but he also has the responsibility to care and protect his people. Against her mother's wishes, I had seven warriors take her in the middle of the night, wrap her in blankets to hide her identity and take her down the river. It took several attempts because she fought the men and none of them wanted to hurt her. Once they were nearly captured by pirates. Eventually, my warriors found a small island. They put herbs in her water to make her sleep and left her on the island." His voice choked and Jimmy looked up from his pad of paper. After a few moments the chief continued, "I asked the Great Spirit to send snakes, my daughter's one fear, to surround the shore and beaches of the island. No man would take her from a solitary island surrounded by snakes. If such a man did exist, I hoped that his courage would win my daughter's heart and hand. No warrior ever proved himself so worthy."

The Chief looked up at Jimmy. "Her rage is my fault," he explained. "Isolation, imprisonment for a lifetime. That is why she went made. That is why her spirit will not rest. In her madness, she has sought the help of living humans to take her revenge on the love she was denied. No living human has dared enter a partnership with her, until now. She has found a way to kill the living and it is my fault."

Jimmy chewed in the end of his pencil and shook his head. "I disagree. I mean, you're a terrible parent," he admitted, "but you're not responsible for murder." He absentmindedly scratched Henri behind the ears as he thought. "Technically, she's not a minor if she's been around for, well," he wanted to be respectful to the Chief, "more than eighteen years. Under state law, you're not responsible if she's older than say seventeen."

Chief Sleeping Bear did not look relieved. "I have created the problem."

Victoria stepped in, "Now isn't the time for placing blame. I think now, we just need to figure out how to stop her before she strikes again."

After dropping Amanda off at the hotel, Ashton drove to DMC hospital where

Raven was listed in critical condition. He followed the map of the large complex given to him by the volunteer at the desk and made his way from one elevator to the next until he reached the critical care unit. There, Ashton flashed his badge at the officer on guard duty and entered Raven's room. His heart stopped.

A teenage girl dressed in a cotton nightgown of sorts was standing next to the head of Raven's bed. Ashton ducked out and went to ask the officer to call for back up. When he spoke to him, the man continued to slump in his chair. Ashton had assumed the officer was reading something on his phone. Ashton shouted and nudged the man. The officer fell over and hit the floor. He stared up at Ashton with stark white eyes. Faint traces of blood dripped from his neck and left hand. He'd been bitten by a snake.

Ashton called out to a passing nurse to call security and the police. There was a murder suspect on the floor. The young man in scrubs ran to the desk and moments later, Ashton heard the PA announcement code for security to come to the fourth floor, critical care tower. With backup on the way, Ashton re-entered Raven's room, gun drawn. He met the girl's white eyes and she hissed at him. Raven's body moved awkwardly under the sheets and Ashton tried to make sense of it as he kept his weapon drawn on the girl.

"Step back away from the bed," he instructed.

She hissed at him like a snake in reply. Her metallic, high pitched voice echoed in the room, "The bargain is struck. No turning back." She uttered words that Ashton could not understand and Raven's eyes, sprung open. He choked and sputtered on the tube in his throat. His back arched. Ashton realized that Raven's body had not been moving strangely moments before. A giant rattle snake poked its head out from the sheet resting on Raven's chest. It struck the man's neck near the artery. Raven's body immediately contracted again. Machines connected to Raven's body began sounding their alarms. Nurses and doctors came running inside but Ashton held out a hand to stop them before they got too close.

"Everybody stay back!" Ashton instructed. He focused his attention back on the girl. "Let's everyone calm down. Is that your pet snake? What do you say we tell him to head on over to the corner of the room and let these nice people help Raven." Raven's body convulsed and white foam dripped from his mouth and ran down his cheek. Everyone in the room watched as his back and neck twisted and then froze. Raven's eyes turned cloudy white. One of the machine's made a single, constant ring where there had once been a blip of a heartbeat. Someone behind Ashton let out a small gasp.

The girl smiled and revealed elongated canine teeth, much like that of the fangs of a snake. Her eerie voice dripped with malevolence. "He takes his place among them. There is no way back." The giant snake slithered from the bed and dropped to the floor. If headed straight for the group of people just inside the door.

"Everybody out!" Ashton said, ready to shoot the animal but unsure whether a bullet would stop the animal. The throng of people rushed out of the door. Security guards unholstered their guns as Ashton reached the hallway. The snake lunged and Ashton jumped backwards. A woman screamed at that was all that it took for one of the guards to fire upon the snake. Several shots later and it lay dead.

Ashton rushed into Raven's room behind the medical team. While the doctors and nurses attempted to revive their patient, Ashton checked every nook and cranny of the room. There was no sign of the girl. He ran out and found one of the hospital security guards. "I need the footage from the video placed on this room. Right now. We have to see where she went or how she slipped out."

"There's no way she could have escaped," the guard argued. "We were all here just outside of the room, in front of the door. Those windows are sealed, double paned and can't be opened for security purposes. There are wires in the frames that set off alarms if they detect fire, extreme heat or breakage. I'm telling you Detective, she has to be in that room!"

Ashton holstered his gun. "That's impossible. You check. I've already looked everywhere."

The guard took out his weapon and proceeded, slowly inside the room to do his own investigation. Ashton watched him from just outside the room, pushing back the curtain on the shower with the nose of his gun, opening cupboards cautiously, swinging a lit in the tiny wardrobe closet. He returned and looked at Ashton in bewilderment. "It's impossible. You're right." Ashton laughed in frustration.

Minutes later, Hank and several police officers arrived on the scene. Hank was out of breath. Ashton shook his head as soon as he saw his old friend. Hank placed a grip on Ashton's arm as he paused to take a breath. "When I heard that shots were fired, I thought," he paused. "Well, I thought the suspect was armed as well."

"She was armed for sure," he cocked his head towards the dead snake in the hallway, "with that thing. It did whatever she told it to."

"And the victim in there?" Hank asked, nodding towards Raven's room.

"Dead," Ashton sighed as he ran his fingers through his hair. "I don't even know how to write up this report. There are some things here I can't explain." His thoughts drifted to Amanda. Maybe she would know. And he needed to apologize. No wonder Victoria came back and tried to warn them.

Hank's radio went off on his belt. "We have an incident at 4279 Woodward Ave. Asking any and all officers to respond, over."

"Anthony," he said to one of the officers, "let dispatch know that we are containing another homicide scene here. We need animal control and the mobile crime lab here stat." The officer lifted the radio to his lips and sent the message.

Hank nudged the dead snake with his boot. "Better you than me," he said, smirking at Ashton. "By the way, the coroner's report came back from the Cumberland murder. She was bitten, but the cause of death was actually smothering."

"Just when I thought we had started to figure some of this case out. I'm afraid it sounds like a different murderer," Ashton hedged.

"Maybe. Or maybe we have a tag team," Hank confirmed. Ashton watched as an officer approached Hank and pulled him aside. Hank sighed as he thought for a moment. "Okay. Take Regis with you. That's all I can spare."

Ashton watched the two officers leave and turned to see the officer who had been on watch duty lifted on to a gurney, a sheet pulled over his body and face. He heard Hank sigh. "That's five total," Ashton confirmed, "and I don't have any. Ore answers today than I did when we first arrived as observers."

"It's one of those days where I don't know where to start and that's just this case. We're going to be two men down because I've had to send Anthony and Regis to the Foundation Hotel to investigate some high holy hell going down over there."

"The Foundation?" Ashton asked with alarm.

"Yeah, I guess some woman called for help and the people next door called management. They just reported a minute ago that there's the sound of breaking glass and a woman screaming. Dispatch just called and said it's urgent. It's in progress now."

Ashton stepped hurriedly away from Hank and dialed Amanda. He held his breath after one ring. His heart started pound through his chest after the second ring. By the third ring, he was heading for the elevator. Her voicemail sounded through his earpiece and Ashton cursed. Inside the elevator he hit the button for the lobby and waited for the beep on the other end of the phone.

"Amanda, it's me. You need to call me right away. If you're listening to this, get out of the hotel." He hung up and shifted to texting. *"Call me. Urgent. Leave the hotel right now. I have my phone in my hand. Just call."*

He sprinted for the Mustang and hit the gas once the engine fired up. Speeding down the road he willed Amanda to hear him. "Come on. Call me. Call me!" The tires squealed as he turned the corner and raced down the road. He hit the button to shut off the air conditioning. The interior of the car was so cold all of sudden. Something caught his attention as he sped down the road. He looked to his right and nearly ran off the road.

"Victoria!" he screamed.

"Hurry, our girl's in trouble. If he wakes her, there's no way back," said the ghostly woman. Then, she vanished.

Chapter 10: No Rest

Amanda read the email Jimmy had sent as she sat at the desk in her room. "Wow, and I thought my teenage years were rough," she said to herself. "At least Victoria didn't banish me to an island; not that she wasn't tempted at times, I'm sure." She looked at the time on her phone. An hour had passed since Ashton left. She tried not to worry. After all, Ashton was the Sheriff back home. Why did helping on a case seem so much more dangerous in Detroit? Guilt bubbled up and burned her stomach. She should have told him about Victoria and what she had said about Raven. But she was a strong, independent woman. She did not need to run to Ashton for every little concern, right? She pushed the worry aside. They'd had arguments before, they'd get through this one as well, she told herself.

To keep her mind busy, she read through Chief Sleeping Bear's statement again. Something nagged in the back of her head. It was as if a big piece of the puzzle was staring at her and she just could not see it. After all, a ghost could not kill a person. The nagging feeling grew. Something Victoria had told her. Amanda thought back to the night at the Ghost Bar in the Whitney. What did Raven do? He was a Collector for ghosts who wanted to do what exactly? Amanda tapped the hotel pen on her bottom lip thinking. What's it that Raven-

"Aww, you're thinking about me," came a voice from directly behind her. She jumped from her chair and spun around. She could not see anything.

"Who's there?" Amanda asked. The room felt electric; as if it might crackle with the strange, new energy that had entered the room. Her phone began to vibrate. It was Ashton. She reached across the desk to answer it and the phone flew across the desk and on to the floor. Amanda gasped as her eyes darted around the room.

Sharp pain spiked across her right cheek as she too landed hard on the floor. She had been hit. She rubbed her face and crawled for her phone. It flew across the floor and under the bed just before her fingertips could touch it. The voice scolded her. "No, no, no," it said. "We're not talking to other people on the phone when there's a guest right here who's come to see you."

"If you want me to talk to you then show yourself," Amanda commanded through gritted teeth. She held her breath and waited. She heard her phone vibrate again from under the bed.

At her feet, the electricity intensified. Unlike Victoria and her cold but gentle mist taking shape, this power swirled and manifest with shocks of pain the closer it came towards Amanda. She screamed as the pain traveled from her feet and up her legs to her torso. "Ah now that's a sweet sound," said the voice. She opened her eyes and there was Raven, or rather what had once been Raven. He had drastically changed.

Amanda stammered, "I thought you were in the hospital. Ashton went to see you."

"Ah yes, you see, I had an offer that I just couldn't refuse. First, I needed to find her a human body, then I had to give her a soul. Once that was done, I could cash in my chips both literally and figuratively, if you know what I mean and take whatever I wanted for myself." He sat down in the chair and touched the glass lamp on the desk. It shattered, raining shards on to Amanda. "While I do have a list of things on my little shopping spree before I head back to my new afterlife digs, I decided that you, my little witch would be the first thing that I would come for. Being a demon can be lonely I'm told. So now I'll have you for, you know, 'company.'"

"Go to Hell," Amanda shouted, kicking at him. When her foot touched his leg, electrical current traveled up her leg and through her body. She clenched her jaws and jerked. With all of her remaining strength, she pulled her foot away and screamed for help. Tears ran down her cheeks.

"Oh, that's exactly where we'll be going. I hope you packed a bathing suit. One that shows off that slender little figure of yours."

He was getting closer. She had to buy time. 'Think,' she told herself. "Before we go I want to know how you did it." She choked back tears. "How did you help Chief Sleeping Bear's daughter escape the afterlife?"

Her question was so filled with specific information that it made Raven stop and smile. "Oh, very good. It's a shame to kill you. You're good at this detective stuff." He sat back in the chair and cross a well-tailored suit pant leg over the other. "You see, I was a Collector. I collect information, power, favors, that kind of thing and I act as a broker, if you will between the living and the dead. The lovely Princess put out a call for a body and a soul. Not too difficult. In exchange, she would offer a quick death and an express track to the demonic realm." He leaned sideways and confessed, "Becoming a demon has always been a dream of mine since I was a kid. So," he sat up in his chair again, "I looked around and found a girl with a broken heart, they're like a dime a dozen; more available than lawyers, really. This one was especially helpful because she already had a connection to snakes, a small requirement that I found in the fine print of the contract."

"So that was the easy part. The tough part was finding a soul. I mean, I'm not man of the cloth and clergy tend to avoid me like the plague. So, what to do, what to do? And then I had it. While everyone has a bit of anger towards their mother, I had what you might call a loathing. In fact, let's say it was a dark loathing of my particular maternal contributor. All that feelings and visions crap. I mean, really. Try living with that line of talk your whole life while you can never really get the scent of patchouli out of your clothes. It drove me mad."

"So, you're the one who killed her?" Amanda managed to ask, willing Victoria to hear her but unsure if that connection could happen without the necklace. She had taken it off so she could concentrate on the police report and not be interrupted.

"Nothing a little snake venom and a pillow couldn't fix. Old 'Mommy Dearest' was dead and gone in a flash and I made it look like our Princess did it. But then she was in too much of a hurry. I called the police about Mom and didn't know the Snake girl had been summoned to complete my contract. If the police had not been so quick, I could have been a demon hours sooner. But no, they had to save me and take me to the hospital," Raven explained, rolling his eyes.

Amanda inched her fingers towards the underside of the bed. She could see the illuminated screen in the darkness. A zap of electricity pierced her chest and she felt all of the air in her lungs escape with the contraction of her muscles. She gasped for air. "I told you, you're being rude," the demon said.

"And I think she told you to go to hell," said a familiar voice. Amanda had never been so happy to hear that voice in all her life.

"Mom!"

"I'm here but you need to get up. There'll be no way out for you if we don't fight together," Victoria instructed.

At that moment, Ashton burst through the door, gun drawn. He fired at the pulsing, crackling Raven. The bullet passed through him and cracked the glass of the window behind him. Raven laughed. Victoria watched Raven ball his fists as if he were to throw a charge at Ashton. She flew to Ashton and blanketed him in cold, ethereal mist. The charge from Raven flew across the room but dissipated as soon as it hit the ghostly mist. Amanda heard Victoria groan but the shield her mother provided held its protective barrier around Ashton.

'I just got them back,' Amanda rallied herself. 'He can't take any of us. I won't let him.' A rage that Amanda never knew she had swelled inside of her. Despite the pain from the intense shocks and the exhaustion from the life Raven seemed to drain from her with every touch, she stood. The rage started in her core and spread down her arms and up her neck into her hands and eyes. Rage, it was the only way to describe it. She had had so much taken from her this past year, so much she had not appreciated but now clung to with her very life. She directed that rage towards Raven.

Invisible yet, growing steadily, a wind erupted from Amanda. Within seconds it was enough to stop Raven's concentration. The electricity aimed at Victoria and Ashton evaporated. Still, the demon looked at her like she was his next meal. His ravenous eyes glowed with red, hot heat. "The little witch has been hiding her secret from me. You'll be even more fun to play with in the depths of hell."

He reached for her, his hand sparking but her power intensified. The shattered glass from the broken lamp, she sheets from the bed and the drapes from the windows joined in the wind that grew in strength and began to swirl. Mastering control, Amanda aimed the tornado at Raven, "Too bad you aren't really a bird," she seethed. "Then maybe you could fly."

The demon gripped the table and snarled, baring his teeth and forked tongue in frustration. "I am a demon. You can't destroy me," he shouted.

"Then, go to Hell," Amanda commanded.

Victoria stood beside Amanda, as mother and daughter began chanting like a coven of two, "We banish you to hell. We banish you to hell." Raven screamed at the words and then vanished.

The tornado made the cracked window explode, glass shattered on to the sidewalk outside. Amanda heaved and tears ran down her face. A gentle voice whispered in her ear, "It's over, Baby. It's over." Ashton touched her arm. His warm breath, the touch of his skin, he was alive. He was safe. "Come back to me, Amanda. Come back to me." Slowly, Amanda let go of the anger and the wind reduced to that of a storm. She took a deep breath and Ashton wrapped one arm gently around her torso. "He's gone. You did it. We're safe now." The wind died down slowly and Amanda eventually set her palm down and closed her eyes. Ashton pulled her close and held her trembling body.

"An Aiolos!" Victoria beamed, clapping her hands together and staring at Amanda with pride. "Wait to I tell Jane Sidway about this! For seventeen years, all I've heard about is how her daughter can communicate with bees. Just wait til I tell her you're a wind conjurer!"

"I think that might have been anger," Amanda admitted.

"Anger, rage, it's got to come out somehow. That's why most witches discover their power when their teenagers. You're just a late bloomer but what a BLOOM!" Victoria said, floating with delight.

Ashton picked a shard of glass from Amanda's hair. "I guess this means your thing won't be enchanted baked goods."

"Sorry," Amanda shrugged.

"It's okay. I didn't need the extra pounds anyways," he said and his smiled traveled from his mouth up to his eyes. "I love you anyways."

Amanda wrapped her arms around him and buried her face in his chest. "If anything had happened to you," she trailed off.

"I can't wait to read this report," Hank said, wide-eyed as he surveyed the damage of the room. "This is the weirdest damned case I've ever seen, and the spookiness seems to dancing with you two. I'd ask you to explain but I don't have time and frankly, I'm too tired."

"Hank, I," Ashton said but Hank held up a hand to stop him.

"Over drinks. A *lot* of drinks," Hank groaned and rubbed his temples.

Amanda felt the cold whoosh of Victoria pass by and knew they needed to talk. "Why don't you and Hank go for a beer while I straighten things out here with management. Besides, we're going to need to move rooms," she paused, "or hotels. Write up the report about the strange man who attacked me," she looked at him with a solemn face, "and then we can meet back to gather our things. Sound good?"

Ashton brushed back Amanda's wild hair and whispered to her, "I don't want to leave you alone. What if that thing comes back?"

"Victoria wants to talk and then we need to figure out how to catch this killer once and for all. With Raven and the killer working together now, their abilities will skyrocket. Take care of Hank and then get back here," Amanda said.

Ashton kissed her on the forehead. "See you in an hour," he said, giving her a wink. A rush of cold fell in the room and Hank rubbed his arms for warmth as Ashton guided him to the hall. He silently moved his lips towards Amanda 'one hour.'

Chapter 11: No Fish in the Sea

Amanda's phone rang and she picked it up quickly. "That was a long hour. Are you okay to drive? Should I come meet you?"

Ashton sounded worried. "I had a ginger ale and convinced Hank to go get some sleep. Did you talk to Victoria?"

"Yes. She, Jimmy, and Chief Sleeping Bear have an idea. If we could lure the killer back to the island, we might be able to exorcize them. We're pretty sure the killer is being possessed by the Chief's daughter and doesn't realize they're committing any crimes. One minute they're in one place, the next minute, they wake up and they're in another. Whoever it is probably feels crazy. We have to stop the Princess before she takes possession of this person and strikes again."

"I think I know who she might be working through," Ashton said. "Dr. Crane has reported her daughter, Zöe missing. I was just going through my notes and Dr. Crane mentioned that her daughter was at a sleepover at a friend's house on the night of the murder. But what if she lied?"

"And in order for possession to take place, the person has to be vulnerable, weak or depressed, like a teenager with a broken heart. Didn't she say she just broke up with her boyfriend and hated people?"

"I don't know. She said more to you than me, but she would have access to a snake or two, "Ashton concurred.

Amanda thought out loud, "Raven was just across the street from the island at his mother's office. If Zöe talked to Raven like she talked to me, he would have known he'd found a host."

"So what do we do?" Ashton asked.

"Victoria has called the full coven to come and help. We'll need all seven of them if we're going to kick Chief Sleeping Bear's daughter out of Zöe's body. They'll be here in about three hours."

"That gives us just under three hours to figure out where she'll strike next. Meet me at the aquarium," Ashton said. "Dr. Crane said she found something that might lead to finding Zöe."

Amanda hung up from Ashton and headed out of her new hotel room. She gripped her pendent right that hung around her neck. "Did you catch all that," she whispered.

The pendent responded by turning cold. Next Amanda dialed Jimmy. He picked up after the second ring. Amanda heard laughter in the background and then Jimmy cleared his throat, "Hello?"

"Uh hi. Are you having a party? I mean, it's okay. You're an adult," Amanda stammered. She thought of how much Henri would hate a bunch of strangers in the house and worried for him. "How's Henri? Is he ok?"

"Oh yeah, he's doing really well. We're just sitting here laughing together watching old reruns of Wild Kingdom," said Jimmy. "The stuff they used to think was family television cracks me up."

"Oh. Ok," said Amanda, not sure how to react.

Henri was laughing?

She pushed the idea aside. "I need a favor. I need you to go into the basement, unlock the trapdoor and look up some books on exorcising someone who's possessed." She paused and wondered if she was saying too much but desperate times called for desperate measures. "Henri can help you. It sounds crazy but he knows his way around books; particularly those books."

"You know I don't really like the idea of going down there," Jimmy said. "I guess if Henri comes with me though. What exactly am I looking for?"

Amanda let the words sink in. 'If Henri comes with him?' What had happened in the few days that she had been away, she wondered. Just photograph the pages from the exorcism pages and send them to me in my Dropbox. Ok?"

"We're on the case," Jimmy said, dutifully. He hung up.

Amanda's Uber arrived at the hotel, and she made it to the aquarium in minutes. Ashton stepped out of the Mustang and waved to her. "I thought you'd be interviewing Dr. Crane by now," Amanda said when she met him on the sidewalk.

"I find you have more of an intuition with people in distress than I do. Dr. Crane is likely to be upset."

He kissed the knuckles of the hand and took a second for his eyes to meet hers. He was searching for any signs of harm from Raven, and she knew it. "I'm fine," she assured him. "Really, I am."

They went to the aquarium door and Dr. Crane stood in the lobby waiting for them. She unlocked the door as soon as they were close enough and scanned the parking lot as she pulled the door closed. "Any word?" she asked, desperately.

"No, Ma'am, I'm sorry not yet. But we've put out an Amber alert complete with her description," Ashton said.

Dr. Crane wrung her hands. "It's because I'm a single mother and I work to much," she said. "I never had much time for traditional family routines. I had Zöe on my own after I finished grad school. I've just taken her with me everywhere I went when she wasn't in school. We've always been close until this year."

"What was different about this year?" Amanda asked.

"Boys. Stupid, idiotic, good-for-nothing boys," Dr. Crane spat.

"Boys? Or one boy in particular?" Amanda asked.

Dr. Crane cocked her head to one side sighed, "I don't know his name. I didn't even know they were a thing until they weren't. And then I found this," she handed Ashton an odd looking piece of paper with writing on it that he could not read. Ashton handed it to Amanda.

"It's birchbark," she said. "It was used as an early form of paper in the Americas."

"Can you make out what's written on it? All I can decipher is Zöe's signature at the bottom on the line there," Dr. Crane pointed to her daughter's signature.

Amanda looked at the makeshift contract. Aside Zöe's name, on the right hand side of the bottom of the paper was a drawing of a black bird. "This looks like a raven," she said, trying to sound calm but willing Ashton to hear the urgency in her voice. Ashton gave her a quick nod to confirm he was thinking the same thing as her.

"Have any rattlers escaped in say, the last few months?" Ashton asked. "I know you said you didn't have a breeding program but would the zoo have any record of any missing snakes, say that bread in the wild without anyone knowing?"

"There's always a certain percentage of loss that the zoo would take into account. Not every egg hatches, that kind of thing," Dr. Crane conceded.

"So, it's potentially possible that there is an unaccounted nest of snakes here on the island," Ashton pushed.

"I suppose it's not impossible," the doctor admitted.

Amanda felt her phone vibrate with an incoming notification from her Drop Box. She sighed. Nothing could be done until the coven arrived. She focused on Dr. Crane. "How did Zöe feel about snakes?"

"Zöe," the doctor's voice cracked with emotion, "she loved anything that crawled, slithered, or swam. She much preferred the company of animals to humans. She hated school because it just took her away from the creatures she loved at my work. Then, this year she brightened. I thought maybe she was finally making friends. I was so happy for her. Then, her counselor called me to say that talk among the kids was that a boy who had seemed to take an interest in her had only done so on a dare. You know a sort of 'I dare you to ask the weird girl out on a date,' kind of thing. Except he took it too far. It was not just one date. She helped him with homework. I looked on her computer and it looks like she wrote several papers for him. He was using her in every way that is cliche and wrong and I had no idea. When he finally broke up with her, it was through text. She locked herself in her room and refused to go to school for three days. I finally took the hinges off of her door and pried it open. You saw how she was after that. I tried so hard to convince her that there would be other boys, other loves, other, I don't know, fish in the sea. I preferred to be alone, but she didn't have to be."

"I'm sorry," Amanda said, consoling. "We'll do everything we can to get Zöe back."

"You think she has something to do with the murders on the island, don't you?" Dr. Crane said more than asked. "She's not like that. She's a misguided and depressed young woman but she would never hurt anyone."

"I don't think Zöe is a murderer," Ashton said softly. "I'll need to take this into evidence, but you'll get it back once the case is closed." He took the contract and put it in a Ziplock bag marked EVIDENCE.

"Thank you for all of your help. We're forming a search and we will update you as soon as we have even a hint of news," Amanda said, touching Dr. Crane's hand and trying to give her a gentle smile.

Amanda's phone vibrated again. It was a text from Mrs. Sidway. "We've arrived."

"Where?" Amanda asked.

"Just over the bridge, of course. We've called Victoria and she's just arrived as well," read the text.

"The gang's all here," Amanda cringed.

"Time to set the trap," Ashton winked.

Chapter 12: No Boundaries

Jane Sidway stepped out of her SUV with three other women. Victoria smiled as she shimmered in her misty glow, approaching them. "I'm my goodness I'm so happy to see you. We have so much to catch up on! But not now, Ashton and Amanda need our help. Where are April and Sophie?"

Jane sighed, "Flu bug. They couldn't come."

Amanda counted the women including Victoria (if you could have an exorcism with the help of a ghost) and herself. "We're one short," she said, crestfallen. She held the phone up for Victoria and Jane to read together. "It says here, according to my book that we need a full coven, seven in total to have enough strength to pull the spirit from the human host."

"Don't you have any friends?" Jane asked.

Amanda rolled her eyes. "You are my friends. And no, I don't have anyone else unless you count Henri and he's not here, oh and he's a cat."

Victoria raised one eyebrow. "It doesn't say that it has to be seven women. It just says seven," a wry smile washed over her opaque face as she eyed Ashton.

He blanched and shook his head, "No Mrs. B. It's not a good idea."

"Just one minute," Victoria countered, using her sternest "mom" voice. "You once said you'd do anything for me."

"Mrs. B! You had cancer. You were dying!" Ashton said, sounding more like pleading.

"And now I'm dead. Would you disappoint my ghost?" she pouted.

Ashton opened his mouth but could not find the words to argue. He stared at the other women who looked up at him, hopefully. Finally, he turned to Amanda.

She shrugged. "There's always a price for eating cakes laced with love potion. Let's face it, you ate a lot of cakes. Time to pay the piper." She patted Ashton on the shoulder, "Welcome to the coven."

"Ladies, we need to spread out and find this missing girl. We think that Chief Sleeping Bear's daughter has possessed her and will strike again tonight, possibly here on the island." The coven members gathered around to look at the picture on Ashton's phone.

Amanda pulled Victoria aside, "Who's watching Chief Sleeping Bear? I thought he was supposed to be with you."

"Oh, he's here. He's pacing, like important men do. I left him on the beach to study the crime scene."

"You don't think that's dangerous, considering the Princess is so angry with being banished to this island?" Amanda asked, incredulously.

"I don't follow, dear," Victoria asked.

"You don't think she'd want a little revenge on dear old Dad" Amanda asked.

"What can she do? The chief has been dead for hundreds of years?" Victoria argued.

Ashton interrupted. "We need to start a sweep of the island."

"I think we need to go straight to the beach. Chief Sleeping Bear is there. I know she can't kill a ghost twice. But the Princess was able to turn a man into demon. Who knows what she might try on a father she's been angry with for over two hundred years."

"Teenagers," Victoria grumbled under her breath.

But when they arrived, they found only the Chief standing on the beach staring out at the sunset over the water. Victoria cleared her throat. "Any sign of her?," she asked.

"She watches me. I can feel her. She has become more than my daughter. She is something else now," he said, sadly.

"She's still in there. The good daughter you raised is still there somewhere," Victoria tried to be encouraging. Amanda held up Evidence Bag for the Chief to see. "Can you take a look at this? Do you know what it says? Maybe it can help."

Chief Sleeping Bear at the birchbark. His expression grew grave and he just shook his head and turned back to the sunset. Amanda stepped forward to argue but Victoria held up a hand to give the spirit a few minutes with his thoughts. After what felt like an eternity, the Chief said, "I know now how great love can be. Tonight, I see that to withhold love, to send it away, to banish it for the sake of convenience, no matter how well intentioned, was the greatest misstep of my life. This agreement says that as Princess of this island, her rule is obsolete. She declares that all true love will be banned from this place and punished by death."

"What about the other name?" Amanda asked.

Before the Chief could answer, Amanda felt the heat of something familiar. Her skin crawled. Her stomach turned to acid. She wanted to scream, to run, but she knew that was exactly what Raven was hoping for. To Amanda's right, she could see Zöe, white eyed, hissing, her hair wild and matted in places. Her white dress was filthy, and her feet were bare. Amanda heard the sound of Ashton's boots crash through the beach grass and Zöe held out a hand towards him. A line of rattlers crowded his next step, lunging at his feet until he took a step back.

Raven fired off a charge that hit Amanda in the back of the legs. She dropped to her knees with a scream, catching herself in the sand with her palms. She heard Raven laugh. "I figured if I can't have you, then no one can; especially the long, tall Texan over there. So, I tricked you by sprinkling my little bread crumbs all the way to the beach. According to this fancy royal decree, Belle Isle belongs to the Princess. She has declared to love is to break the law." He leaned in a little closer to Amanda and touched her jawline making her wince with the light electrical pain he induced. "Bet you wish you'd taken my offer of hell. If you don't wish it now, you will," Raven hissed. Amanda instinctively went to raise a hand but looked down to find a rattler had slithered both. It rattled its tail in warning and Amanda froze, hoping her lack of movement would keep it from feeling provoked and striking. She was bound like a dog to the sand.

Chief Sleeping Bear spoke to his daughter in a language Amanda could not understand. The Princess spat back. Amanda did not have to understand their language to know that they were on opposite sides of the argument. They had been played and the Snake Princess had outmaneuvered them. Amanda looked from the corner of her eye. The women of the coven were acting spells of protection on Ashton and edging him away from the serpent line in the sand. It gave Amanda one desperate idea.

"Mother, it's no use. They've got us. You should take Chief Sleeping Bear and the rest of you seven and go." She emphasized each word, praying that Victoria understood the message. She then twisted her head up as far as she could to address the Princess.

"It's true. I do love Ashton. If you kill us both, remember that I'm a witch. I'll find him in the afterlife. We'll be together for eternity. You will give us what we want. But if you spare him, leave him here alive while you kill me, then, well, I'll be like you. I will be stuck in a world to which I was banished, and my heart will be broken. Is that what you want? You want to make every lover feel as miserable as you've felt all these years?"

"Don't try your mind games with me, witch," the Princess whined, her voice echoing down the beach, one part human, one part combined metal and water. "Raven will have your soul in Hell once I kill you."

"Thank you, your Majesty," Raven bent low and stepped towards Amanda as he did so. The snake at her hand slithered slightly. She had one chance, and it was a long-shot. She dared not move, not yet, not until she was sure that Victoria and the coven were in place. She had to stall.

"Zöe," Amanda called out. "Zöe your mother loves you. She's looking for you. She's worried. I know you feel trapped, but you have to fight. You have to push this ghost away from you, push her out of you."

The Curse of the Snake Princess

The Princess screamed. Her face became a serpent itself. Her lips peeled back to expose her fangs. Her eyes turned jet black with a yellow, elongated iris. Amanda wondered if it was her imagination, or did Zöe's neck elongate to make her look more serpentine? The Princess bellowed out to the sky and Amanda took her chance.

With lightweight speed, she yanked her hands out from under the snake, grabbing two fistfuls of sand as she did. With the sand in her right hand, she threw it directly at the snake's at her level's eyes, hoping to temporarily blind it. With the handful in her left, she threw it in Raven's face, hoping for the same result. She jumped to her feet and ran towards the blissful sound of chanting. The coven. The women, Ashton and Chief Sleeping Bear made seven, and hopefully a strong enough number to save Zöe.

She glimpsed behind her and saw Ashton try to break away, let go of the hands of the man and women in the circle. Amanda shook her head. She wished she could explain. She was only buying time. They were doing the real work. Amanda raised her hands up and called the wind from four corners. She asked for their cooperation. The wind complied. As it gathered around her, she used it to pick up some of the sand. Raven had taken her slow start as an invitation to strike, throwing a ball of glowing electricity at her. She jumped and sent the ball back with her power. Unfortunately, Raven just caught it and played with the ball of energy like a toy. He tossed it in the air and caught it a few times.

"I really to love that you like to play," Raven licked his lips, looking at Amanda like snack. His monologue was cut short, much to Amanda's relief when the Princess screamed and gripped her chest. The skin of the possessed girls' face rippled as if something were crawling around under it. Her neck cracked. He hips shifted to the extreme right, twisting the girl's spine.

The coven chanted, this time, Amanda looked over and they were all in sync. Ashton even had his eyes closed. Raven raised his ball of electricity to throw in their direction, but Amanda blasted him with sand, wind and debris. She concentrated, make the wind swirl again but this time, the tornado was wide. As she sent it closer to Raven, it opened its funnel like a gaping mouth and swallowed the demon. The hollow force of wind enclosed around Raven on all sides and held him. She watched with amusement as light and orbs of color reflected and bounced off the walls of Raven's cage.

As she held off Raven, the chanting sent the snakes away from their circle. They protectively slithered to their mother, the Princess. She tried to console them, caressing them with her fingers, holding some of the ones who crawled up her body and around her neck.

"It's not working," Amanda heard Jane shout. "We have to surround her if we going to get her out of that poor girl. Everybody run!" Free of the chance of being bitten, the Snake Princess's line of defense had retreated to their source. Ashton, the Chief, Victoria, Jane, Eliza, Georgia, and Susan ran to the beach and rejoined hands once they surrounded the girl.

Zöe and the Princess eyed them menacingly. She threatened them, she cursed them in a language not even the Chief could understand. "Don't listen to it," Victoria instructed. "Just focus on my words. Let them drown her out. With that they started again. This time, they were a united force, hand in hand, chanting in unison. Zöe screamed and beat her fists in the sand as she dropped to her knees. To Amanda's horror, a rattle snake bit the girl.

Another set of boots came crashing through the grass, breaking Amanda's concentration. It was Dr. Crane. The woman ran for the sacred circle. Amanda had to decide: stop the mother who did not understand what she was seeing, or keep the demon caged. As Dr. Crane got closer to breaking the exorcism, Amanda dropped her hands and ran to stop her.

"They're splitting them apart. You can't interfere!" Amanda shouted and held back the woman.

"They're hurting her," cried Dr. Crane.

"Not as bad as you'll hurt before I'm done with you," roared Raven.

Dr. Crane screamed as the demon's entire body exploded in a burst of rage inspired energy. He threw ball after ball and bolt after bolt at the two women who unsuccessfully tried to run quickly in the sand. Amanda fell and she looked to see that Dr. Crane had fallen just a yard or two away from her. She heard the woman screaming and crawled across the sand, she raised a hand, hoping the wind she could conjure might act like a shield, but Raven had grown more powerful in his anger. Amanda felt an electric belt of pain sizzle and burn the skin around her waist and pelvis. She heard herself scream. She clawed at the sand as she rolled on to her back.

Blackness and exhaustion began to blue the edges of Amanda's vision. She had to admit, as she listened to herself and the woman beside her cry in agony, she did want to die. She would try hell just to stop the torture. Death might be peaceful. Hell did not sound fun, but maybe she would not go there. She was a witch. She did not believe in a heaven or hell described in books. If she did not believe in such places when she was alive, her electrocuted brain reasoned, why would she be subjected to its rules when she was dead?

She gasped what she wondered might be her last when she felt something odd under her sandy palms. Glass? Had she been struck so hard by one of Raven's revenge-seeking bolts that it had turned the sand near her to glass? No, she confirmed. This was pliable. With all of her strength, she willed her brain to make one more deduction. She opened her eyes in the narrow scope of her vision to see what her desperate and burned hand had discovered. She rolled on to her side and there in her fingers was the contract in a very torn, very singed Evidence bag.

Victoria's words flooded her ears. "They're separating. We're splitting them apart. Don't stop!"

"In two," Amanda mumbled through cracked, burned lips. "In two," she said again, and sand crunched between her dry gums and teeth. With strength she did not know still lived inside of her, she rolled onto her side, her blistered fingers shook as she reached her red singed hand into the bag and pulled. Touching the paper felt like a thousand needles burrowing into her skin but she persisted. She thought of only one word.

Splitting.

Her second hand joined her first and they began to tear the birchbark contract. For the first time in an eternity of agony, the electrical pulses stopped. Amanda sucked in air, unaware until that moment that she had not been breathing. It improved her vision slightly. She ripped a ribbon off the thick, ancient parchment. In response, Raven stumbled backwards.

Encouraged, Amanda ripped away a larger ribbon, cutting the contract one third apart. Raven fell to the ground and gripped the skin of his face. Another cry from just beyond Amanda's vision told her that Zöe and the Snake Princess were apart. Hurriedly, Amanda shredded the last of the contract in jagged ribbon pieces and threw them to the water. The tide licked them, saturating them and drawing the ink into the Detroit River and away from the bark.

When the last letters of Raven's picture signature had washed away, Amanda watched in horror as claws and giant meat hooks erupted from the sand that surrounded the Collector. One clawed hand gripped the man's leg followed by a hook that plunged deep into his body. The demon howled. One after the other, his limbs were secured to some invisible platform. Slowly and silently, Raven was swallowed alive by the shifting sand.

Chapter 13: No Goodbyes

Ashton handed Amanda a coffee, placing it gingerly into her burned but bandaged hand. "Any news while I was downstairs," he asked.

Amanda stared at the coffee for a minute and nodded. "Dr. Crane has been taken to the burn unit but she's stable. She'll make a full recovery."

"And Zöe?" Ashton asked with far more trepidation in his voice.

"No," Amanda whispered. "The antivenin was too late." She put her hand delicately in his. "You saved her soul or whatever it is that leaves this place, but her body just wouldn't fight anymore."

Ashton let go and rested his head in both hands. "She was too young." Eventually he sat back up and put his arm around Amanda. "What did Victoria say about the Princess?"

"The Chief took her home, again wherever that is, whatever that means. She's been freed from the island either way which means she won't be making deals with Collectors and possessing heartbroken teenagers any time soon."

Ashton looked at Amanda's bandaged hands. "Some romantic getaway I planned," he scoffed.

"You sure know how to show a girl a good time," she laughed.

"Seriously, I'm sorry. Let's throw our phones in the river, go back to the hotel and eat room service for the next three days. My treat," Ashton offered.

"On a Sheriff's salary? Do you realize what the last hotel bill is going to cost you? Besides, you know what? We accomplished what we set out to do."

"Solve a super creepy case that once again I'll have to lie about in a report?" Ashton asked, shakily.

"No," Amanda confirmed. "We wanted to know each other better, share some time together in bed." She paused because she could feel the heat filling her cheeks. "I believe we wanted to find a way past the grief. In a way, we did all of those things."

"I suppose. I mean don't get me wrong, the bed part was nice but when were you going to tell me you caused the Wizard of Oz, little Miss Tornado?"

"That was news to me too," Amanda admitted.

"So once you left your grief behind, you found your power," Ashton surmised.

"Or maybe once I let myself really fall in love, I discovered another new part of myself," she suggested.

"Fell in love? Anybody I know," Ashton teased.

Amanda leaned her whole body into his chest. "Can we just go home?"

"A little over a year ago you couldn't wait to leave that house," Ashton reminded her.

"A little over a year ago I didn't have you and I couldn't understand Henri and I didn't get along with Victoria. Now it's a house, its home. And I think it's high time we shared it, if you're willing at least a couple nights a week."

"Amanda Burton, do you know how few people live in our town? If I stay a few nights a week, they're going to say that we're living together. Sounds like scandal to me," he said, but in his eyes, he meant none of it. He kissed her long and slow. When he pulled away, he looked puzzled, "What do you mean understand Henri. Are you telling me you speak cat too?"

"I can't tell you all of my secrets in one weekend. You'd get bored. You're a detective and you need to investigate things," she said it smiling but there was a little mischief in her tone.

Ashton's phone rang and he let it ring again, choosing to return the mischievous smile back to Amanda before he picked up on the second ring. "Sheriff here, what's up Jimmy?"

"I have a question but I'm not sure if it's for you or Amanda," Jimmy confessed. "Are there police cats?"

"Excuse me?"

"I know there are canine units so I just wondered if we might try having a feline unit?"

"What's wrong?" Amanda whispered.

Ashton put his hand over the receiver of his phone. "Sounds like Jimmy's bonded with the cat this weekend. He wants to know if he can bring him to work."

Amanda laughed, "Henri hates the car. He'd never get him past the front door."

"Jimmy," said Ashton, "Amanda and I think a feline unit is a good idea, but you'll have to find a way to get Henri to agree to ride in the car. Amanda says he hates it."

"I'll call you right back," Jimmy replied and hung up.

Amanda gave Ashton a puzzled look. "I don't know. He said he'd call back." Ashton leaned in to kiss Amanda when his phone chimed. He gave the phone a sideways glance. When he looked closer, he squinted and tapped the screen.

"What?" Amanda asked. "What is it?"

"You're not going to believe this, but I think Ironwood has its first patrol cat," Ashton said and turned the texted picture Jimmy sent towards Amanda.

She blinked as she stared. The picture was of Henri seat belted in his travel backpack with his face happily looking out the top of his glass bubble. The caption read, "Deputy Henri has already assisted in the apprehension of three shoplifters who fled the scene of the crime. You can read all about it in my report." Amanda returned her gaze to Ashton in disbelief.

"Sure you don't want to stay a few more days in Detroit?" Ashton teased. "I hear there's a screaming banshee downtown somewhere…"

And now here's a sneak peek at the next Michigan Macabre Mystery!

The Plague of Nain Rouge

Chapter 1

Penelope had not been called to the emergency room since her residency days. What could be so terrible that the Emergency doctor on rotation could not handle it? Wednesday was her long day in surgery. She had finished late, sent the nanny home, made dinner and fell into bed after reading bedtime stories and checking homework. She was awoken by a frantic ER nurse that she was needed stat.

Nurses did not frighten easily. They were tougher than most doctors and nothing scared them; especially after Covid. They'd steeped in death, watched in horror as some of the first patients drowned in their own lung fluid and held cell phones up while loved ones said good bye. What could be worse than all of that , on repeat for months on end?

Penelope held up her badge to Frank in security and passed through the staff entrance of the hospital. She quickened her pace as she rounded to the reception desk. Joe, a college intern sat at the desk typing frantically while attempting to process a very full emergency waiting room. Penelope tucked her coat under a shelf and hit the security button that opened the door to the ER. A nurse ran up to her and covered Penelope's face with a mask.

"I'm not sure if we have a live virus or what, wear this to be safe," Karen instructed.

"If you're worried, just isolate the patient. Hell, roll them into a broom closet until you get blood work back,' Penelope barked. "What's with the drama?"

"We did isolate but we're running out of room."

"What? Who's on-call tonight?"

"Uh, well you are now," Karen hedged.

"No, no, no. I'm a surgeon."

"You're next in seniority," Karen explained. "I double checked before I called you."

"Where's Christopher, err, Dr. Manning?" Penelope asked.

Karen continued to show Penelope to an old X-ray room they used for housing large equipment. Scanners, large medical carts and ultrasound machines sat outside the door. "He's here, doctor."

Seven beds lined the room with makeshift curtains drawn across and oxygen tents and machines running. Penelope adjusted her mask and then pulled the curtain to Christopher's bed. She stared in shock at her friend, who was barely recognizable. She snapped herself to attention and hurried over to the shelf near his bed and clicked on his digital chart, reading impossible numbers and lab results. She turned back to get a closer look.

Christopher's face was deep red, nearly the color of a beet but his temperature nor his blood pressure indicated that it should be. His hands were red too. Penelope looked closer at Chris's left hand where a wedding band rested just above grossly elongated fingernails. "His teeth and ears," she heard Karen whisper.

Penelope checked to make sure Chris was unconscious, calling his name and lifting his eye lids. He irises were jet black. She lifted his upper lip. Chris's teeth had changed. Instead of a dazzling G.Q. smile that often led him to do spots for the hospital's marketing department, he teeth were small and pointed. His ears were misshapen.

"How long has he been like this?" Penelope asked.

"All seven came in from lunch about eleven. About an hour later, they just started collapsing one by one. None of them are conscious." Penelope set Chris's hand down and examine each staff member one by one. Several were doctors, a couple were interns, the rest were nurses and physician's assistants.

The door creaked open and an old woman moving her own wheelchair started to enter. Penelope shouted at the woman, "You can't be in here. These people are in quarantine!"

"Nain Rouge been here," said the woman in a thick Creole accent. "Trouble's comin'. Bad trouble in on its way. When Nain Rouge show up, it means that the devil himself is on his way…"

<u>Other Books by Michele Roger</u>

The Michigan Macabre Mysteries
Terror Under the Lupin Moon
The Curse of the Snake Princess

and more:

Eternal Kingdom: A Vampire Story
The Harpist
Huggy Muggy Do! (as Michele Roger-
Beresford, with Finnegan Dudley)

About the Author

Michele Roger is a harpist, writer and teacher. She's also a mother and a grandmother. She grew up speaking French with her grandmother as a child and continued on reading and writing in the language, later writing music for children in French.

Michele is the author of "Terror Under the Lupin Moon", "Eternal Kingdom: A Vampire Story," "The Conservatory," several short stories, including "Just Like Dolls," and children's stories "Huggy Muggy Do," and "The Harp and Storm Tamer."

She has also written non-fiction books for adults, including "Contemporary Wedding Ceremonies for the Human Race."